Dates
and

Sole
Survivors

Cathy Hopkins lives in North London with her handsome husband and three cats. She spends most of her time locked in a shed at the bottom of the garden pretending to write books, but is actually in there listening to music, hippie dancing and talking to her friends on e-mail.

Occasionally, she is joined by Molly, the cat who thinks she is a copy-editor and likes to walk all over the keyboard rewriting and deleting any words she doesn't like.

The other cats have other jobs.

Barny likes to lie on his back in the grass, stare at the clouds and create poetry. (Sadly, none of it has been published, as it has been hard to find someone to translate it from Catspeak, but he and Cathy are ever hopeful.)

Maisie, the third cat, was worried that Cathy may have forgotten what it is like to be a teenager, so she does her best to remind her. She does it very well. She ignores everybody and only comes in to eat, sleep and occasionally wearily say 'miwhhf' (this means 'whatever' in Catspeak).

Apart from that, Cathy has joined the gym and spends more time than is good for her making up excuses as to why she hasn't got time to go.

Mates, Dates and Sole Survivors

Cathy Hopkins

PICCADILLY PRESS • LONDON

Big thanks to Brenda Gardner, Yasemin Uçar and the team at Piccadilly, for all their support and feedback. To Rosemary Bromley at Juvenelia. And Alice Elwes, Becca Crewe, Jenni Herzberg, Rachel Hopkins, Annie McGrath and Olivia McDonnell, for all their emails in answer to my questions.

First published in Great Britain in 2002
by Piccadilly Press Ltd.,
5 Castle Road, London NW1 8PR

Text copyright © Cathy Hopkins, 2002

A catalogue record for this book is available from the British Library

ISBN: 1 85340 727 5 (trade paperback)

9 10

Printed and bound in Great Britain by Bookmarque Ltd
Design by Judith Robertson
Cover design by Helen Allen, Artpix Design

Set in 11.5pt Bembo and Tempus

The quotation on page 166 is credited to Irina Dunn.

Chapter 1

Summer
Hols

'This has to be the best feeling in the world,' I said to Nesta as we walked out of the school gates on the last day of term.

'I know,' she said. 'Six weeks with no Miss Watkins . . . Six fabola weeks with Simon before he goes off to uni.'

'And six weeks with Ben for me,' said Izzie linking her arm with Nesta's. 'We're going to work on loads of new songs for the band now we'll have time.'

'And I suppose we'll be seeing *you* round at ours a fair bit,' I said to TJ. She's been seeing my elder brother Steve over the last few weeks and they're both completely smitten.

'What about you, Lucy?' asked Nesta. 'Going to give *my* poor brother a break at last? You've been giving him the runaround for months now. I don't think his ego can stand much more of it.'

Six weeks with Tony? The idea was appealing and I reckoned I was finally ready for a 'proper' relationship with him. We'd liked each other for ages and we had gone out for a while earlier in the year, but then I broke it off as it felt like it was all happening too fast. After that, there was a lot of flirting between us whenever I saw him round at Nesta's and he did ask me out again a few times, but I turned him down. It's not that I didn't want to date him. He is gorgeous and funny and I love his company, it's just that he has A Bit Of A Reputation when it comes to girls. Nesta had warned me that it was a different one every week at one time. She says he likes the chase, then drops them the minute they show they're interested. So I had to play it carefully, or else by now, I'd be on his long list of rejects and broken hearts. But it had been almost nine months since I met him and he did keep trying, saying I was the only one for him, the lurve of his life. I thought, I can trust him not to mess me about.

I grinned and pulled an envelope out of my rucksack. 'I know,' I said. 'I've been doing a lot of thinking about him lately. And I've finally come to a decision.'

'Which is?' asked Nesta.

'I've written him a card. Saying no more messing him about. I really like him and we're on on ON.'

'About time,' said TJ. 'I don't know how you've been so cool for so long. I think I'd have fallen at his feet the first time he asked me out.' Then her face clouded. 'Um, that is, er, I don't mean I would steal him or anything, I'm just saying I think he's gorgeous.'

I squeezed her arm. 'I know what you mean, TJ. But boys like Tony enjoy a challenge.'

'Well, what is it?' she said. 'Eight . . . nine months you've made him suffer? I reckon that's enough challenge for any boy.'

'I can hardly believe it,' said Izzie. 'Last year, none of us had boyfriends. Now this year, we all have.'

'It's not definite yet,' I said.

'This time last year, I hadn't even been kissed,' said TJ.

'And now there's no stopping you,' teased Nesta. 'Snog Queen of North London.'

This time last year, I hadn't been kissed either. Tony was my first. That's another reason I wanted to take it slow. I didn't want to get tied to the first boy I'd snogged. I wanted to try a few others and see what they were like. There have been a few others now. No one important or serious. In fact, no one who's come close to Tony. He still has the same effect on me every time I see him. My stomach turns over and I get all hot and my face goes pink.

'You're not just doing this because you'd be the odd one out?' asked Izzie, pointing at my letter.

'But I *am* the odd one out,' I teased. 'You're all tall and dark with long hair and I'm small and blonde with short hair.'

'No. *I'm* the odd one out,' insisted Nesta. 'I'm the only one with dark skin.'

'No, I'm the . . .' started TJ.

'I *meant* the only one without a boy,' interrupted Izzie.

'No, course not,' I said. 'I think I'm ready now and I want to see where it goes. To tell the truth, I started thinking that maybe I was messing him around and playing him along because I was scared of rejection. You know what he's like . . .'

Izzie nodded. 'Yeah, and you're right. You can't let fear hold you back.'

'I've been reading this book,' said TJ. 'It's by this guy called DH Lawrence and it's about a posh lady who falls for her gardener.'

'Oh, Mills and Boon?' asked Nesta.

I laughed. Typical Nesta. Her idea of reading is flipping through *Bliss* or *Now* magazine. TJ, on the other hand, devours books – proper books. That's why she gets on with my brother Steve. He's a bit of a brainbox as well.

'Um, no, not Mills and Boon,' said TJ, 'but it is a love story. *Lady Chatterley's Lover,* it's called. Anyway there's one line I really like. Want to hear it?'

We all nodded.

'I can't remember it exactly,' she said, 'as I didn't write it down, but it's something like: better a life of risk and chance than an old age of vain regret.'

'Yeah, cool,' said Nesta. 'I'll buy that. You don't get anywhere in life unless you go for it.'

'Feel the fear and do it anyway,' said Izzie, quoting the title of one of the self-help books she loves so much.

'So what did you say in the card?' asked Nesta.

'That's Lucy's private business,' said Izzie, 'Don't be so nosy.'

Nesta looked offended and poked her tongue out at Izzie. 'I wasn't. I was feeling the fear and asking my question. You don't find out anything if you don't ask what you want to know. So . . . go on, Lucy, tell us what you said.'

I knew the note off by heart, because I'd written and rewritten it so many times. I wanted it to sound right – cool but romantic, so he could keep it as a memento to look back on.

'I did it like one of those Japanese poems,' I said, 'you know, the ones with only three lines that we did in English last term. Haikus.'

'Bless you,' said Nesta.

'*No,*' I said. 'The poems. They're called haikus.'

'Whatever,' said Nesta. 'So what did you write in your hiccup?'

'I'm not changing, I'm just rearranging, my life to be with you.'

'Ahh,' said TJ. 'That's really sweet.'

'Yeah,' said Izzie. 'You should come and help the band with our lyrics. So what else did you put?'

'Then I wrote, "Sorry for messing you about over the last year, but now I'm ready. I know we have something really special and I want to make a go of it. Call me." I wanted to keep it light, you know?'

'Sounds perfect,' said TJ.

I took a deep breath and, as we passed a post box, I popped the card in. 'Me and Lady Chatterley. No old age of vain regret for us. I've put a first class stamp on, so he should get it in the morning. Gulp. No going back now.'

'It'll be fine,' said TJ. 'I think you'll make a fab couple and we can all do loads of things together – play tennis, go to movies, it'll be great.'

'OK,' said Izzie, 'so that's Lucy sorted. But there's more to life than boys. Let's make some other goals for the summer holidays.'

Typical Iz. She's always setting herself goals and targets, then insists that we do as well. She says it's important to think about what you want in life, then visualise it happening. I visualised me with Tony having a great time. My first proper relationship. It would be top. No worrying about whether you were going to pull or what boys were going to be where. And, did you really like him and did he really like you? Will he phone or should you phone him? . . . It would be good to be settled for a while. All of us. We could all just enjoy being with each other, hanging out as couples and no one having to worry that anyone was on their own.

'*So?*' said Izzie, looking at us all when we reached the bus stop. There's no arguing with Iz when she's off on one of her 'Let's improve ourselves' campaigns. 'Come on. Resolutions for the summer hols?'

'Resolutions are for New Year,' said Nesta, tossing her hair back. 'You make them on January first then give up on them around January tenth.'

'OK, I've got four,' I said. 'Number One: Hang out with you lot as much as poss. Two: You already know now – Tony *et moi*. Three: Stop blushing.'

'I think it's lovely that you blush,' said TJ. 'It's really sweet.'

'Noooo,' I said. 'It's horrible. I feel so stupid and everyone stares like I'm a kid.'

'No one ever really notices,' said Izzie. 'And Number Four?'

'I'm going to make T-shirts,' I said. 'Like those ones on sale in Camden Market. You know, the ones with cool slogans on them.'

'So what are yours going to say?' asked TJ.

'Don't know yet. I'm going to start collecting good lines over the hols.'

Just then the bus came, so all discussion was stopped while we piled on. It felt great to be alive. School was over. The sun was shining. The evenings were light until ten o'clock. I'd finally taken the plunge and posted my card, and I couldn't wait to get his reaction.

'What's for dinner?' I asked Mum when I got home.

'Tofu burgers, broccoli and rice,' she said, looking up from the counter where she was chopping onions. 'Want to give me a hand?'

Yuck, tofu, I thought, as I threw down my rucksack in the hall and went to join her. I wish she'd cook normal stuff sometimes. My dad runs the local health shop, so we always eat what he brings back. I know it's good for you and you are what you eat, etc., but my secret fantasy is to come home one night and discover it's chicken nuggets, baked beans and chips. It's funny because the way we eat is *Izzie*'s fantasy. She loves health food, tofu and soya and quinoa. Sometimes I think we got the wrong parents. Izzie would love to live here; in fact, she almost does, as she comes round so often. Me on the other hand, I like living here, but I'd love to have supper at Nesta's. Her dad's Italian and does the most amazing pasta dishes, and her mum's from the Caribbean and her spicy fish and peas is to die for. Amazingly, Nesta is as thin as a rake. I think if I lived at her house, I'd be enormous, so maybe it's a good thing I have strange parents who make peculiar meals.

Suddenly I thought of a good resolution for the holidays.

'Mum, how about this summer, *I* cook supper a few nights?'

'Sounds good to me,' replied Mum, grinning.

'Can I get the ingredients as well?'

'Sure,' said Mum.

Just at that moment, the phone rang. 'Whatever I want?' I asked as I went into the hall and picked up the receiver.

It was Tony.

'Hi,' he said. 'What you doing later?'

'Nothing,' I said. 'Nothing for six whole weeks. We broke up today.'

I decided not to say anything about the card. I wanted it to be a surprise when he opened it in the morning.

'Fancy meeting up?' he asked. 'I wanted to talk to you about something.'

'What?'

'Not on the phone. I'll meet you at Raj's in Highgate, say, in half an hour.'

'Hold on, I'll just ask Mum,' I said, putting my hand

13

over the receiver. 'Can I go out for a bit? Promise I won't be late. I'll wash up when I get back.'

'How can I refuse when you put it like that?' Mum called back. 'I'll put your supper in the oven for you.'

'See you in half an hour,' I said to Tony.

I put the phone down feeling a rush of anticipation. I knew what he wanted to say. He feels the same way I do and wants to make it definite, I thought, as I dashed upstairs and changed into my jeans and a T-shirt. A slick of lip-gloss, a squirt of the Angel perfume the girls got me for my birthday, then I ran out and caught the bus up to Highgate. I felt so excited. As I sat on the bus, I decided that I'd let him say what he wanted to say and I'd be cool about it, like, 'Oh, I'll have to think about it'. Then tomorrow, he'll get my card and realise that I wanted the same thing as him all along. It was all working out so perfectly.

He was already upstairs at Raj's when I arrived. He was settled in the corner seat reading one of the ancient books they keep stacked on the shelves there. He looked up and smiled as I walked in and, as always when I see him, my stomach did a double flip.

'Had your hair cut,' I said.

'It's called a French crop. Like it?'

I nodded. Not many boys can take their hair that short,

I thought. You have to have good features and the right-shaped head. Of course, Tony had both. Good looks run in his family. Nesta is easily the best-looking girl in our school and Tony is probably the best-looking at his. Dark, with sleepy brown eyes and long lashes.

'Take a pew,' he smiled, as I slid in behind the table. I smiled back. We always said that when we went there, as the chairs are all old church pews.

'Want some tea or something cold?'

'A Coke would be good,' I said, as I looked around. I was glad he'd chosen this place to meet. It's TJ's favourite place as well as mine. She says she always feels as though she's in a novel from another era when she comes here as the decor is kind of Bohemian. It's different from all the other cafés in the area – it has its own character, with the pews and heavy wooden tables and bookshelves heaving with interesting books.

'What you reading?' I asked.

Tony pointed at the bookshelves. 'Oh, some ancient history book. They have a weird collection here, a real mixture, from cookery to Dickens. All the books look about a hundred years old.'

I nodded. 'Like the nick-nacks,' I said, pointing to a chipped statue of an Indian Maharaja on the corner unit above Tony's head. It had been plonked next to a statue of the Buddha. 'In fact, it's a bit like our living room at home with all sorts of junk that doesn't really go together.'

'Yeah,' said Tony, indicating two brass trumpets that were hanging from the ceiling. 'It is a bit mad. But I think that's why I like it.'

We spent a few minutes chatting about all the strange ornaments we could see – the Russian dolls and toy ostrich on one shelf, brass flamingos and ceramic elephants on another, the old sepia photographs on the wall mixed in with some framed ink sketches. I felt so comfortable sitting there with him that I thought it would be difficult not to spill the beans about my card and my Decision.

'So, you had something you wanted to say?' I finally asked.

'Er, yeah,' said Tony, as the boy behind the counter left his computer and came to take our order. 'But first, tell me how you are? Broken-up, huh?'

I nodded. 'Best feeling in the world.'

'So what you going to do with the holidays?'

I knew it. He was going to ask if I'd go out with him.

'Oh, no definite plans,' I said, looking into his eyes in what I imagined was a meaningful way. 'Got any ideas?'

Tony shrugged. 'Not really. That is, um, Lucy . . . How can I put this . . .?'

I longed to reach out and take his hand, tell him that I knew what he wanted to say and that I felt the same. But

Nesta had trained me well. Stay cool. Don't be too easy.

Tony took a deep breath. 'Thing is, Luce, well, we've been on and off for ages now and I wanted to get things straight between us. It's not fair on you and it's not fair on me. We've got the holidays ahead of us and it's like a new chapter, for both of us, so . . . so, what I think is that, er . . . maybe we should make a clean slate of it.'

'Clean slate? What are you saying?' I didn't understand.

'Well, it's not like we're boyfriend and girlfriend, are we? We never really have been.'

'No. No, course not.' Was he going to ask me if I *would* be now?

'And I was thinking,' Tony continued, 'what if, say, you meet someone this holiday or I meet someone? It's kind of confusing. Our situation, that is . . . me and you. Well, we're not free and we're not really committed.'

'No, we're not.'

'So, what do you think?' he asked.

'I'm not sure I understand,' I said. 'Are you saying you want to be committed or that you want to meet some-one else?'

Tony shifted awkwardly. 'That I want to be free,' he said finally.

'You're dumping me?' I blurted.

'No. No, course not, how can I dump you when we were never going out properly?'

'But . . .'

He reached for my hand, but I snatched it away. I felt hurt. Confused.

'Look, Lucy, it's not as though I haven't asked you out in the past, but you always put me off.'

'I didn't know how I felt then,' I blustered. 'It wasn't that I was putting you off, but . . .'

'I'm not dumping you. I'm getting it straight, so we both know where we are. We can still be friends.'

Friends? I knew exactly what the 'We can still be friends' line meant. It means, that's it. *Finito.* The end. I didn't want to be *friends* with him. I didn't want to hear about him being *more* than friends with anyone else. I looked across at his wide sensuous mouth. No more snogging that mouth. I felt the back of my eyes sting. I was going to burst into tears, but I didn't want to do it there. For him to see how upset I was. 'Got to go,' I said, getting up.

'But what about your Coke?' I heard him call as I reached the door and stumbled down the stairs.

'You have it,' I muttered over my shoulder. I only had one thought in my head as I rushed home. Got to phone Nesta and get her to catch the postman tomorrow morning before Tony sees that stupid stupid *stupid* card.

Chapter 2

Gooseberry Fool

I called Nesta the minute I got home.

'She's not here,' said Mrs Williams. 'Do you want to leave a message?'

'Um, no thanks,' I said. I knew Tony might see it when he got home, so leaving a message was definitely a no-no.

I quickly dialled her mobile. Murphy's Law. Nesta who *always* has it switched on, had it switched off.

I left a message on voice mail. 'Nesta this is *urgent*. You *must* intercept that card I sent Tony. Whatever happens, he mustn't get it. Call me ASAP.'

Then I texted the same message. Then I emailed it. It would be all right as long as he didn't read the card. But if he *did* . . . The thought made me feel queasy. All that stuff about how we had something special. Oh, arrghhhh. And wanting to make a go of it. Double arrrghhh.

I lay on the bed and groaned.

Mum popped her head around the door. 'Are you going to come and have your supper, love? I saved some for you.'

I shook my head. 'Not hungry.'

Mum looked at me with concern. 'You OK?'

I shook my head then nodded. 'I'm fine, just not hungry yet. I'll heat it up later. Promise.' I didn't want to talk about it. I was too embarrassed. Dumped. I'd been dumped and we weren't even having a proper relation-ship. How sad is that? I needed to talk to Izzie. Wise old Izzie, she always knows the right thing to say.

Luckily, Mum knew better than to push it. She's good at knowing when to leave me alone. I guess it's partly because she works as a counsellor and is used to dealing with people that are freaked out but can't talk about it. She's always saying that you can't force people to open up when they're not ready.

'Come down when you want. No hurry,' she said and shut the door.

When she'd gone, I dialled Izzie's number.

'Isobel is round at Ben's,' said the lodger. He's not really the lodger. He's Izzie's stepfather. She didn't get on with him in the beginning, so she nicknamed him 'the lodger' to help her cope. They get on better now, but the nickname stuck.

I tried Izzie's mobile. Also switched off. What is the point of having a mobile if you don't keep it turned on? It's so annoying. I keep mine turned on all the time. Except in the cinema, of course. It's maddening when one of them goes off in the middle of a film.

My mobile rang. At last, I thought, as I picked it up. Must be Izzie or Nesta.

'Hey Lucy.' It was Tony's voice.

I panicked. I didn't know what to say. He was the last person I wanted to talk to.

'Lucy, are you there?'

I hung up. I felt like someone was strangling me. I didn't want Tony to know how upset I was and I didn't know how to play it. Not until I'd talked to one of the girls.

The phone rang again. I switched it off in case it was Tony calling back. I felt numb and confused and was just wondering what to do next, when I heard a familiar voice in the hall outside my bedroom. Oh, thank God, I thought, as I opened the bedroom door.

'TJ!' I cried. 'Thank God you're here.'

'Why, what's the matter?' she said.

I was just about to launch in when I saw that Steve was standing behind her. Of course, I thought, she'd come over to see him.

22

'Er, nothing,' I said. 'Just . . . it doesn't matter . . . You carry on.'

TJ turned to Steve. 'Won't be a mo.' Then she pushed me back into my bedroom and shut the door. 'What's going on?'

I slumped on the bed. 'Oh TJ, you can't imagine,' I said, and filled her in on the whole story.

She listened quietly. 'I'm so sorry,' she said. 'You must be gutted.'

I nodded.

'I know it may feel awful at the moment,' she said, 'but you don't know what or who's round the next corner. Remember what happened with me when I had that thing about Scott next door? I felt awful when it wasn't working out, then it turned out to be the best thing ever. He wasn't worth it and I met Steve. Who *is* worth it. Maybe it just wasn't meant to be with Tony.'

I groaned. I knew she meant well but it wasn't what I wanted to hear. 'But it was different with Tony . . .'

'I know,' she said. 'Oh Lucy, I wish I knew what to say.'

A knock on the door disturbed any further conversation and Steve stuck his head in. 'Come on, TJ, I've got the Amazon website up, I'm waiting for you.'

TJ looked anxiously at me.

'You go,' I said. 'I'm fine, honest.'

'You sure? Because I can stay here with you,' she said.

Steve looked at me as though that was the *last* thing he wanted.

'No, honest. Go.' I didn't want to ruin everyone's night just because mine was turning out to be crapola.

'Why don't you come and join us?' asked TJ, looking at Steve for agreement. Which he didn't give.

I shook my head. Dumped and a gooseberry in one night. No thanks.

'All part of life's rich tapestry,' I said, quoting one of Mum's favourite lines. 'I'll get over it, and besides, I have loads to do. You go.'

I got up and began to tidy away things in my room.

'Don't worry,' said TJ. 'Nesta will get the card. It will be OK.'

'Yeah right,' I said. 'Me and Bridget Jones. It's cool to be a singleton. Don't worry, one day my D'arcy will come.'

As she shut the door, I thought, But Tony's my D'arcy, isn't he? Or is he the bad boy character played by Hugh Grant in *Bridget Jones's Diary*? Oh, I don't know.

Mum always says that things seem better after a good night's sleep and I did wake up the next morning feeling slightly more positive. At least that's what I told myself. It's not as though Tony and I were having a proper relationship. Then I looked at the clock. Ohmigod. It's nine-thirty.

Nine-thirty. Ohmigod. *Ohmigod*. Did Nesta get my message? Did she get the card before Tony did? I checked my mobile, and oh *no*, I'd forgotten to switch it back on after Tony'd called last night. There were three messages. One from Tony asking me to call him. One from Izzie asking me to call her. And one from Nesta asking me to call her.

I quickly found my dressing-gown and ran downstairs into the kitchen.

'Why didn't you wake me, Mum?'

She looked up from the table where she was reading the paper. 'It's Saturday, Lucy. And you seemed a bit low last night. I thought I'd let you sleep in . . .'

'Did anyone call?'

'Izzie. She said your mobile's off and she'll try later.'

'You should have woken me.'

Mum sighed. 'I can't win, can I? Usually if I wake you early at the weekend, I'm wrong, and now I *don't* wake you and I'm wrong. I give up.'

I ran back upstairs and called Nesta's number then hung up. Tony might answer. I dialled her mobile number.

Phew, I thought, when she answered.

'Lucy . . .' she began.

'Did you get the card?'

There was an ominous silence.

'Oh Nesta, *please* say you did.'

'Oh Lucy, I got back late last night and I've only just

listened to the messages on my mobile this morning. And
. . . and the postman's already been.'

'Has he got it?'

'Tony? Yes. I saw him take a card into his room. But
what's the problem? Why did you want me to get to it
first? Did you change your mind about wanting to see
him over the holidays?'

'No. *No*. He's changed *his* mind. We met up in Highgate
and he told me he only wants to be friends . . .'

'I'll kill him.'

'No don't, Nesta. But find out how he reacted to the
card. Oh pants. Oh, and Nesta, *try* to do it in a subtle way.'

'Yeah, course. But I think we need to meet up.
Urgently. I already said I'd meet Izzie later this morning.
You phone TJ. Ruby's, eleven-thirty?'

'Fab,' I said. 'Thanks. And tell me everything Tony says.'

'Every last detail.'

Ruby in the Dust is Nesta's favourite café. It's by the
roundabout in Muswell Hill and is even funkier than
Raj's. The sofas and tables are so well-worn they look like
they came off a skip, but it gives the place a cosy, lived-in
feel. Loads of local teenagers hang out in there, us included,
most weekends.

The girls were all there when I arrived and they looked
up at me anxiously when I walked through the door.

'You OK, Lucy?' asked Nesta, as I sat beside her on a sofa in the window.

It was then that I spotted Ben. He was at the counter ordering drinks. What was he doing here?

'Do you want a cappuccino?' he called.

I nodded.

'Sorry,' mouthed Izzie. 'I didn't know what it was all about until Nesta told me just now.'

'And Simon's coming too,' said Nesta, looking sheepish. 'I tried to call him to put him off, but he'd already left.'

Oh great, I thought. And I suppose my brother's coming too. I looked over at TJ. She shook her head.

'Steve's at football this morning,' she said.

'Yeah, course,' I said. He played every week. I was bursting to ask if Tony had said anything about the card so turned to Nesta quickly before Ben came back.

'So?'

'He didn't say much. Just that he'd got your card and that it was private. I didn't let on that I knew what you'd written. He asked me to ask you to call him.'

'Is that everything?'

Nesta nodded.

'Honest?' I asked.

'Honest,' she answered. 'And I didn't hit him or anything. Though I'd have liked to.'

'So what should I do?' I asked, looking around.

'Try to stay friends,' said Izzie.

'No. You must *never* speak to him again,' said Nesta.

'Maybe I shouldn't have given him such a hard time,' I said. 'Maybe it's my fault.'

'Rubbish,' said Nesta. 'You were too good for him. You deserve better.'

'You'll find someone else,' said TJ.

I looked around the café. There were a few boys there and, as always, they were all ogling Nesta. She did look stunning in her denim shorts and a cut-off T-shirt, with her hair loose like silk all the way down her back.

'No. No one will *ever* look at me again,' I groaned,.

'Rubbish,' said Izzie. 'You mustn't let this dent your confidence.'

'Find someone else, settle down and have a really committed relationship. That will show him,' said TJ.

'No, *no*. Last thing she needs,' said Nesta. 'Have some fun. Go out with *loads* of boys. Play the field.'

'*No*. You need some quiet time,' said Izzie. 'Time to heal.'

'No, no. Fill your diary. Keep busy – you must keep busy,' insisted Nesta.

I couldn't help but laugh. 'D'oh, thanks girls. Now I'm really confused.'

As Ben came back with the coffees, the café door opened and Simon came in. Some of the boys in the café looked peeved when they saw him make a beeline for Nesta, who smiled and kissed him. Of course the boys being there put an end to any discussion about Tony, so I did my best to act happy and not let Ben or Simon see how freaked out I really was.

After we'd drunk our cappuccinos, Simon suggested that as the weather wasn't brilliant, we go to the early show of a movie. I wanted to go home and hide under my duvet but Nesta insisted that I go as well and there's no arguing with her when she's made up her mind about what's best for someone. TJ will be there, I thought. So it's not as though I'll be the only singleton.

'Um, I said I'd meet Steve after football,' said TJ, getting up and looking anxiously at me. 'I can cancel if you want to do something.'

I shook my head. 'Don't be mad. I'll go to the movie.'

I didn't like this kid-glove treatment they were giving me, like I was ill or something. The last thing I wanted was my mates feeling sorry for me. Oh, poor Lucy, she's been dumped. Poor Lucy sent a romantic card to someone who's not interested. I'd show them I was fine. So they've all got boyfriends and I haven't, I thought. No biggie. I'm not going to let it get to me.

At the cinema, Nesta and Izzie insisted that I sat in between them rather than on the end. It was OK at the beginning and I was glad I'd gone with them. No one can see that you're on your own in the dark. We were just five teenagers watching a film.

That is, we were until Ben put his arm round Izzie and they cuddled up and Simon went into a snogathon with Nesta. I felt a right twerp, sitting with a straight back in the middle, giant tub of popcorn on my lap that no one was eating except me. The only one really watching the movie. I tried to focus on the film and forget about Tony and boys and what was happening on either side of me, but the film was a romantic comedy. Oh, arrggghhh, I thought, as the screen hero moved in for a snog. Arrrghh, *arrrghh*. Snogging to the left of me, snogging to the right. And snogging in front of me, in glorious magnified technicolour on the screen. No escape.

I'm not doing this again, I thought.

Chapter 3

Solo
Sundays

The next day, I decided I'd hang out with my brothers. It seemed a good idea, as in term time it's like we're just lodgers in the same house. Eat, queue for the bathroom, fight over what's on telly, go to bed, go to school, pass on the stairs. I'd spend what Mum calls 'quality time' with them.

'Do you want to do anything after lunch?' I asked at breakfast time.

'Busy,' said Steve, peering at me over his glasses. 'Meeting Mark for tennis. Sorry.'

'Harry and Edward are coming over after lunch,' said Lal. 'We're going to discuss our summer strategy for pulling girls.'

'Oh, get a life, Lal,' I said. 'Don't you ever think of anything else?'

'Yeah, food,' replied Lal, spreading peanut butter and honey on his toast then ramming it into his mouth. 'Need to keep up my strength for all the top totty.'

'Dream on, dorkbrain,' I said. 'Who in their right mind would look at *you*?'

'Get lost, toadbreath,' said Lal. 'Loads of girls fancy me.'

'Quality time with them? Well so much for that plan,' I said to Mum, as Steve and Lal scoffed down their breakfast then scarpered off to their rooms.

'Life is what happens to you when you're busy making plans,' she said. She's always coming out with stuff like that.

'Yeah right,' I said, thinking about my plan to spend the summer with Tony. 'Tell me about it.'

I've got three choices, I decided, as I went upstairs to my room.

1) Mope and be miserable;
2) Find another boyfriend;
3) Find an interesting alternative.

I decided to go for option three. Moping and being miserable would be a waste of time and the precious holidays. As Mum says, life is not a rehearsal. You only get one shot at it so make the most of it. And the thought of option two, looking for another boy just to make up the numbers with Nesta, Izzie and TJ, was too gruesome. I'm not that desperate and I don't need a *boy* to be happy. Having a boyfriend can be exciting and fun, *if* it's the right boy. It can also be heartbreaking, humiliating and confusing. So, good alternatives?

I tore a sheet of paper out of my notepad and sat on the bed. Right, I thought. Nice things to do when you're single. A list:

1) *Eat chocolate.*

Good idea. In fact, I'll get some right now.

I took a quick break from the list to go and raid the cupboard downstairs. Only organic in this house of course, but Green & Black's is pretty good.

2) *Shop.*

Got no money, so cross that out for the time being.

3) *Movies.*

I could go on my own, but as I discovered yesterday, all that's on at the moment are romances. Or boy's films, and I'm not in the mood for watching people blow each other up in space.

4) *Little treats, like a manicure, pedicure or facial.*

That's a good idea, I decided. I'll have a beauty day.

★ ★ ★

I spent the next few hours pampering myself. I painted my nails with my strawberry-scented glitter polish. I did a papaya facial. I took a long foamy soak with passion fruit bath gel and exfoliated my whole body, including elbows and knees, with citrus and ginger exfoliator. Then I washed my hair with Mum's apple shampoo, rinsed with fresh lemon and then conditioned with peach afterwash.

Then I was done. Beautified. I smelled like a fruit bowl. Now what? It was one o'clock and the day was starting to feel *very* long.

Life is what you make it, I thought. Clearly I needed a hobby.

I went down into the kitchen where Mum and Dad were preparing Sunday lunch.

'I need a hobby,' I said. 'Any suggestions?'

'But you have your sewing,' said Mum. 'All those T-shirts you're making.'

I nodded. 'Suppose, but they don't take long to make.' It's true I do like sewing, as ultimately I want to be a fashion designer, but I wanted to try something new.

'You could walk the dogs more often,' said Dad, gesturing towards the garden where Lal was having a pre-lunch cavort with Ben and Jerry, our two golden Labradors.

35

'Could,' I said. 'But I can't manage both of them on my own.'

'Get some goldfish,' said Dad. 'I'll get you a tank.'

'Um, no thanks,' I said, sensing he wasn't taking this very seriously. I remembered last time we had fish. No one ever wanted to change the water, so they only lasted a few weeks.

'Take up jogging,' said Steve, coming in from the living room.

'Ever seen a happy jogger?' I asked. I certainly hadn't. Loads of people do it and they all look miserable, red in the face, puffing, but with a determined look in their eyes. Not my idea of fun.

'Well, there's all sorts of exercise you could do,' said Mum. 'Cycling, swimming, dancing, skating, judo, rowing, aerobics . . .'

It was beginning to sound like the extra curricula classes at school. I pulled a face.

'Well, I don't know Lucy,' said Mum. 'What do you *want* to do?'

'Something new,' I said. 'Something I can do on my own.'

'Ah, is this our new independent Lucy?' said Dad. 'You could come with me the week after next. I've been invited to a workshop in Devon. It's run by a friend of mine. I'm sure she'd be glad to have you along as well. You wouldn't be on your own, but it might do you some good.'

'What sort of workshop?'

'It's a kind of rejuvenation workshop. Yoga, self-help classes, therapy, learn to de-stress, getting to the root of problems.'

'Sounds like Izzie's sort of thing, not mine,' I said. Izzie was well into anything new age. If ever any of us caught a bug or fell ill, she always had an explanation for it. Like when Nesta got a sore throat, Izzie asked her what wasn't she saying that was blocking her throat. And when TJ hurt her knee, Izzie said that it was because she wasn't willing to bend. It was hilarious, though, when her mum got a boil on her bum and Izzie told her that it was because she was sitting on her anger. Literally, we all thought. There might be some truth in it, but personally I'm all for taking someone a bunch of daffodils when they're ill and giving some good old-fashioned sympathy.

'How many psychotherapists does it take to change a light bulb?' asked Mum.

'Dunno,' we said.

'One,' she said, grinning. 'But only if it really wants to change.'

Dad laughed out loud. I suppose that's an in-joke for people that work in counselling and therapy . . . and their husbands.

'How many Spanish people does it take to change a light bulb?' asked Dad.

'How many?' said Mum.

'Juan.'

'Want to know the very first light bulb joke?' asked Steve.

Mum nodded. Typical, I thought. Trust Steve to know the original joke. He's a mine of useless information from reading all his books. Though I suppose he would be a good person for 'Phone a Friend' if you were on *Who Wants to Be a Millionnaire*.

'How many Chinese people does it take to change a light bulb?' he asked.

'How many?'

'Millions. Because Confucius say, many hands make light work.'

Steve, Mum and Dad fell about laughing.

'Look,' I said, 'we were discussing a hobby for me. Not telling light bulb jokes. I've got six weeks and *nothing* to do.'

'Oh, poor Lucy,' said Mum. 'Now let's think. There must be something for you.'

'Loads of things,' said Steve. 'Read, learn to cook . . .'

'Excellent,' said Mum. 'In fact, you were going to cook for us one night.'

'Garden,' said Dad. 'Those beds outside need a turn over and the weeds need pulling out.'

'Learn a language,' said Steve.

'Learn to play an instrument,' said Dad. 'Violin or piano. I could teach you guitar.'

'Take up photography,' said Steve.

'That's *your* hobby,' I said.

'Trainspotting,' said Lal, coming in from the garden. 'Stamp-collecting. Are we playing a game? Who can name the most daft hobbies?'

'Something like that,' I said, as visions of me in an anorak, watching trains or digging up worms in the garden filled my head.

Luckily, I was saved from any more of my family's brilliant suggestions by the phone ringing. It was Nesta.

'Help,' I said. 'My family want me to take up gardening.'

'I have a better idea,' said Nesta. 'I've been thinking. There are plenty more fish in the sea besides my ratfink brother. I've been talking to Izzie about it and we have a new mission.'

'Which is?'

'Mission Matchmake. Lucy, *we* are going to find *you* a boy. And not just any boy. The perfect boy.'

Even though I'd dismissed that from my list earlier that morning, somehow it seemed a more appealing alternative to stamp-collecting or taking up knitting.

'You're on,' I said.

Mission
Matchmake

Nesta called first thing the next day.

'Mission *Numero Uno*. Place: Hollywood Bowl,' she said, going into sergeant-major mode. 'Outside Café Original. Time: three o'clock.'

'Do we need to synchronise our watches?' I asked.

'Yes, good idea,' she replied, not realising that I was joking. 'See, the plan is to catch the boys either going in to the movies or coming out, so we need to find out the times of the films. Coming out is probably better as they'll hang out for a while afterwards and give us time to assess the situation and the talent.'

'Yes sir,' I said.

Just for a joke, I wore my combat trousers and khaki

T-shirt, but Nesta didn't pick up on it when I arrived at the cinema.

TJ did, though, and laughed. 'Ready to do battle, Lucy?' she asked.

'Private Lucy reporting for duty,' I said, saluting. 'Has anyone brought binoculars?'

'Or camouflage gear,' laughed Izzie, getting into it. 'We could smear our faces with mud then hide in the bushes with a bit of tree stuck on our heads.'

Nesta tossed her hair. 'You may laugh, but coming here is a good strategy. See, look – there are loads of boys around.'

Nesta was right. It was a good place to start, as Hollywood Bowl is a popular haunt for most North London teenagers. Apart from the cinema, there's a bowling alley, a pool, and a variety of assorted cafés all built in a square around the car park. Today, as always, there were groups of teens hanging out in the sunshine in front of the cinema.

'Looks like we're not the only ones on the pull,' said Izzie, watching the groups of teens all eyeing each other up.

'I am *not* on the pull,' I said. 'It sounds desperate when you put it like that. I don't want a boy just for the sake of it.'

'Course you don't,' said Izzie. 'We're only looking.'

'How about we say that we're doing research?' said TJ.

'I saw some girls doing it on one of those "How to get a date" programmes on telly. The presenter said that a good way to meet boys was to pretend that you're doing a survey and ask them a list of questions. It's one way of getting talking to them.'

'That would be a laugh,' I said. 'Anyone got any paper?'

The girls all shook their heads.

'I think we'd need a bit more than paper if anyone was to take us seriously,' said Nesta, looking at what we all had on. Izzie was wearing a T-shirt and denim mini, TJ and Nesta had shorts and T-shirts on and I was in my combats. 'Not exactly dressed like professionals, are we?'

'We'll do that another day,' I said to TJ. 'And we'll dress the part.'

'Now, let's see who's here. Don't look as though you're looking,' said Nesta, casually glancing round the car park. 'We don't want to be too obvious.'

'So how am I supposed to check the talent?' I asked.

Nesta turned her back away from the groups of boys then got her mirror out of her bag. 'Like this,' she said. 'See, it looks like I'm checking my hair or something but actually I'm looking behind me.'

Izzie and I got our mirrors out and lined up with Nesta to try out her technique. TJ shared mine with me and I couldn't stop laughing as we watched the people behind us.

Nesta sighed. 'I give up,' she said. 'You lot are just a wind-up.'

'Sorry, Nesta,' I said, putting away my mirror. 'I do appreciate this, honest I do. And I get what you're saying – look kind of casually.'

I glanced at the boys, then over to the left, like I was looking for someone in the distance, then back at the boys, then over at the cinema.

'Perfect,' said Nesta. 'That's the way to do it. Now, check out left, by the pillar, jeans, black T-shirt. Guy with blond spiky hair.'

'Not my type,' I said. 'Too . . . um, too hair-gelly.'

'OK, left, dark, French crop. Wearing all black.'

'Yee-uck,' I said, looking over at the boy. 'Do me a favour. He's picking his nose.'

'OK, I got one,' said TJ. 'Behind spiky boy, dark.'

'Where? . . . Oh yeah,' I said, catching sight of him. 'Yeah, he's a possibility.'

'He's checking you out, Lucy,' said Izzie.

I glanced over. 'Ohmigod, he's looking at me. I think he knows we're talking about him. Ohmi*god*, he's coming over.'

'Excellent,' said Nesta. 'Now play it cool, look away, don't let him know you've noticed him.'

Of course I went bright red. A dead giveaway, if ever there was one.

The boy came straight up to me. 'Hi,' he said. 'Can I talk to you a minute?'

I glanced at the girls, who were all grinning like idiots and giving me the thumbs-up behind his back. I couldn't believe it. Success so fast. And he was cute. Very cute, like Enrique Iglesias.

He led me behind the pillar and looked deeply into my eyes.

'That girl you're with . . .' he began.

He didn't have to finish. I knew what he was going to say immediately. It's not the first time this has happened. Boys always fancy Nesta. And no wonder, she is stunning and a half.

'The dark one?' I asked.

'Yeah. Has she got a boyfriend?'

'Yes,' I said. 'In fact, all those girls I'm with have got boyfriends.'

He looked disappointed. Not as disappointed as I was, though. He didn't even bother to ask if I was attached.

'Never mind,' he said. 'Thanks.' Then he shuffled off.

I couldn't help feeling a tiny bit jealous. I do love Nesta – she's a great mate – but it's hard sometimes, being the last one that anyone notices. I went back to join the girls, who looked at me expectantly.

'Wanted to know if you were taken or not, Nesta,' I said. Nesta looked over at the boy. 'Really?'

Izzie smacked her arm. 'We're here for Lucy, not you. Besides, you have Simon.'

'I know,' she said. 'But no harm seeing what I'm missing.'

'Let's try somewhere else,' I said. 'Any ideas, anyone?'

'How about Hampstead?' said Izzie. 'There's always loads of boys there.'

'Lead the way,' said Nesta, heading off towards the bus stop.

'But please, let's just hang out, look in the shops and forget about the Mission,' I said. 'I don't think it's going to work. It doesn't feel right. I mean, so there might be a boy who looks OK, but how am I going to approach him? Get a card with "Hi, I'm Lucy and I'm available" on it? Besides, I'm always reading that the right boy always comes along when you've given up.'

'No,' said Nesta. 'You have to make things happen.'

Izzie shrugged. 'No, Lucy may be right, Nesta. You can't force destiny.'

'Choice not chance determines destiny,' said Nesta. 'You can't leave everything to fate or the stars.'

Oh, here we go again with the conflicting advice, I thought. It's amazing Nesta and Izzie get on at all. They both think so differently about things. If Nesta said 'hold on', Izzie would say 'let go'. They never agree on anything. Chalk and cheese. Still, it seems to work on some strange level. Opposites attract and all that.

'What do you think, TJ?' I asked.

'No harm in looking,' she said. 'It's like window shopping. Good to see what's on offer, but it doesn't mean that you have to buy.'

I liked that perspective. It took the pressure off.

We caught the bus down to Hampstead where everyone was sitting, sipping cappuccinos and enjoying the sunshine outside the cafés that line the streets. After trawling the pavement for a while, looking for an empty table, we finally ended up outside the Coffee Cup. All the tables were full except for one that was occupied by a boy sitting on his own and reading. He looked nice and there were three empty chairs next to him.

'Anyone sitting here?' asked Nesta, pointing at the chairs.

The boy smiled and said, 'Nope, only me. And Jesus.' He then pointed at the book he was reading, which turned out to be the Bible. 'Please, sit down. I'd like to tell you how you can be saved.'

Izzie was all for it, as there's nothing she likes more than a discussion about religion and why we're here and stuff. But luckily Nesta had a better idea.

'I really fancy ice cream instead of coffee,' she said, making a beeline for the ice cream shop next door.

'Good idea,' I said following her. 'When the going gets tough, the tough need chocolate chip fudge.'

Wish
List

I decided I needed to rethink the plan. Mission Matchmake had left me feeling more aware than ever that I was single. Nesta and Izzie, however, weren't ready to give up. Nesta wanted me to go out boy hunting again in Kensington on Tuesday with her and Simon, but I said I was busy helping Dad out at the shop. I didn't want to hang around with her and Simon, like a spare part. And I didn't want Simon thinking I was desperate. Because I'm really *really* not. Of course, Izzie heard about my refusal to go out and came over to see me on Wednesday.

'I don't want to pick up any old boy. I want it to be special, like it was with Tony.'

'Then what you need to do,' said Izzie, 'is to send a

message out into the universe about what you want, then you'll attract it to you. You should do a wish list for a boy, then wrap it in tissue, put it in a secret box and hide it in your bedroom.'

'If it's going to go out into the universe, wouldn't a billboard up at Swiss Cottage work better than hiding a piece of paper in my bedroom?' I teased.

She gave me 'the look'. The one our form teacher, Miss Watkins, gives when someone hasn't done their home-work.

'Trust me,' she said. She was always coming up with ways to make things happen or control your destiny and stuff. She's got one of those spell books at home, and when Tony was coming down with a case of the wandering hands last year, she told me to put a photo of him in the freezer to cool him down. I laughed at the time, but maybe it worked after all. He'd certainly gone cold on me now.

I stretched out on my bed while she took her favourite place on the beanbag on the floor. 'OK, mystic Iz. So what's a wish list?' I asked.

'You have to write down all the things that you want in a boy on one side of the paper, then all things that you have to offer on the other side.' She got up and found a pen and piece of paper from my desk and handed it to me. 'Start with how you want him to look, then go on to personality – like funny, generous, that sort of thing. Then emotionally and spiritually how you'd like him to be. The more detail, the better. Leave nothing out.'

Why not? I thought. I had nothing else to do and it was better than being made to go out and trawl North London like a saddo.

'OK,' I said, and began to write.

My perfect boy:
Medium height, not too tall. Fit-looking. Nice face.

'Blond or dark?' asked Izzie, coming to sit on the bed next to me and looking at what I was writing.

'Um, don't mind really, as long as he's quite nice-looking.'

'Oh, go for it,' said Izzie. 'Write drop dead gorgeous. Cute. Don't settle for just anyone.'

Gorgeous-looking, cute, long eyelashes. With nice hands and nails. Clean. Well-dressed, with a sense of style. Interested in fashion.

'Now you're getting it,' said Izzie. 'Now his personality.' I continued writing.

Reliable, i.e., will phone me when he says he will.

'Excellent,' said Iz. 'But what else? Just reliable could be a bit boring.'

Good fun to be with. Sense of humour. Really likes me.

Honest. Doesn't play mind games. Not afraid to show his feelings about me. Intelligent. Ambitious. Kind. Sensitive. Spontaneous. Likes animals.

'Good,' said Izzie. 'Now do you.'

I turned over the paper. 'Um, don't know what to put,' I said.

'Blonde, small, slim,' dictated Izzie. 'Am fab at fashion. Have my own sense of style. Am honest. Have a great sense of humour. Am generous. Sensitive. Spontaneous. Am a great friend to my mates. Am punctual. Sweet.'

'Sweet? Eeeww. Boring.'

'No, it's not. And you *are* sweet,' said Izzie. 'When you want to be.'

'How about: Have Wonderbra, will travel?' I added.

Izzie laughed. 'Have inflatable bra, will travel.'

Nesta and Izzie bought me an inflatable bra ages ago when I was fed up about being so flat-chested. It's on the notice board in my bedroom, pinned under a photo of me taken when I was twelve.

'Maybe I should put on his side that he likes girls who have boobs like peanuts,' I said.

'Put: Likes petite,' said Izzie. 'Sounds better.'

I added that to his side of the paper, then as Izzie instructed, I wrapped the paper in tissue and put it in my Chinese box in the drawer in the bedside cabinet.

'Excellent,' said Izzie. 'Now let's see when he turns up. It may even be on Friday. It's Ben's birthday and his parents are letting him have a party at his house. He said to invite you and Nesta and TJ. You will come, won't you?'

'Are Simon and Steve going?' I asked.

'And Lal,' Izzie said. 'But there'll be loads of other boys there. It'd be amazing if perfect boy turned up.'

I laughed. She really believed in her hocus-pocus.

'Course, I'll come,' I said. 'It might be fun.' I had to admit that a part of me was secretly hoping that Izzie's wish list would work. I had nothing to lose by going to find out.

All the girls looked stunning at the party. Izzie was wearing a white peasant top, a denim ruffle skirt and cowboy boots, Nesta was in a blue strappy slip dress and TJ was in jeans, but she was wearing a fab turquoise halter-top.

I wore an outfit I'd made a few weeks before. It was a tight red corset basque that laced down the back and a black taffeta skirt. And I wore a bright red lipstick to go with the corset. I felt really good. Really in the mood for flirting.

'You look amazing,' said Izzie to me. 'Sexy.'

'Thought I'd better make an effort in case dreamboy's here,' I laughed.

'You look like a character out of *Moulin Rouge*,' said TJ. 'Really suits you.'

'Thanks,' I said, doing a quick scan of the room. On first glance, dreamboy was nowhere to be seen. There were loads of boys there, but not one who came close to fitting the bill. There was a thin, dark-haired boy in the corner and I could see he was eyeing me up, but I turned away. Definitely not my type, though it was nice to be noticed.

As the party got going, it soon became clear who was in a couple and who was single. In the front room, someone changed the music to a CD of love ballads and some of the couples got up to drape themselves round each other and smooch-dance. I decided to go and investigate the rest of the house and practise my flirting, but every room I went into seemed to be full of couples snogging. The front room, the hall, the little conservatory at the back of the house, everywhere. The singletons present mooched about from room to room trying to look as though they were having a great time but I could tell that some of them felt like I did. Like we had neon signs over our head saying 'SINGLE'. The only person there who seemed to be enjoying being single was Lal. So far, I'd seen him snog two different girls, one in the hall and one on the landing.

'It's quality not quantity,' I told him when he came up for air between girls. 'Do those two know about each other?'

He grinned. 'Course not.'

'And don't you ever think about their feelings?'

'Oh, get off my case, Miss Prissy Knickers,' he said. 'Chill out. You take it all way too seriously. You should be more like me. Enjoy. We're young, we're free, we're single.'

'I don't want to be like you. I do actually want to feel something for the people I snog,' I said.

'Why? You're missing out, I tell you,' he said, as he spotted a small dark girl who looked a bit lonely. 'Anyway, got to go. So many girls, so little time.'

'Seen anyone you like?' asked TJ when I went into the kitchen to get a drink.

I shook my head.

'There's a few more boys upstairs. Why don't you go and have a look?' she suggested.

I traipsed up the stairs behind her. A crowd of lads were in Ben's bedroom playing a game on his computer. I glanced over at them then shook my head.

'No thanks,' I said, and turned to go back downstairs. 'They all look like they're up past their bedtime. Way too young.'

It was then that I saw him. He was coming in the front door and he was drop dead *gorgeous*. A tingle went through me. Dreamboy most definitely, I thought.

It was Tony.

I drew back and sat on the top stair so that he couldn't

see me, then watched him through the banisters. There was someone with him. A willowy girl with long blonde hair. She was very very pretty. He took her hand and led her into the kitchen. No wonder he wanted to be free for the holidays, I thought. Free to go out with her.

Nesta came racing up the stairs a moment later. 'Ohmigod,' she said. 'I'm sorry, Lucy. I didn't know he was coming. Do you want me to ask him to leave?'

'No. *No*. Course not. He'd think I was pining after him,' I said. 'I'll keep out of his way. It'll be fine. How long has he been seeing her?'

Nesta shrugged. 'New one to me,' she said.

'Well you can't stay up here all night hiding,' said TJ. 'Look he's gone into the kitchen. Come down and go in the front room and Nesta, you go and distract Tony.'

I followed them down, but suddenly I wasn't in the party mood anymore. What was the point of practising my flirting on boys I definitely had no interest in? I could hear Tony talking in the kitchen and laughing. Oh hell. What was I going to do?

'Get off with one of the boys,' said TJ, coming in to the front room to join me. 'Act like you don't care, show him that you've moved on as well.'

I looked at the assorted gangly boys on offer and shook my head. 'Nah, I don't want to get into playing games just to get a reaction from him. Look TJ, I'm going to go home. I'll just slip out. Tell the others I've gone.'

Izzie got up from the sofa where she'd been sitting with Ben.

'You need to sort it out between you and Tony,' she said. 'Otherwise, it's always going to come back and ruin your peace of mind. Lucy, for your inner happiness, you *have* to clear up anything unfinished.'

'Yeah right,' I said and headed for the front door.

When I got home, I thought about what Iz had said as I left the party. Something about finishing everything that's left unfinished in your life. She was right. That's exactly what I needed to do. So I finished off a tub of Ben & Jerry's, a packet of Rolos and a packet of double chocolate chip cookies.

Somehow I don't think those were the sort of things she had in mind.

Chapter 6

Family
Advice

Mum brought me a cup of tea in bed the next day.

'You all right, Lucy?' she said, sitting down on the end of the bed.

I nodded. 'Sort of.'

'Good party last night?'

'Sort of,' I said.

'Usual crowd?'

'Yeah, and a load of Ben's mates.' I sat up and took a sip of the tea, then decided to fill her in. '*Everyone* has got a boyfriend except me.'

'So what happened to Tony? I thought he was your boyfriend. Sort of.'

'He's got someone new. He was there with her last night.'

'Oh Lucy, poor you. Was it horrible?'

'Sort of.' I felt my face start to crumple. It always makes me blub when people are nice to me. I'm weird like that.

'Sort of,' said Mum. 'Makes a change from whatever. Want to talk about it?'

'It's just . . . all week, TJ and Nesta and Izzie have been on a mission to find me a boy, but . . .'

Mum nodded. 'You don't want just any boy?'

'Exactly. Going out looking for one only made me more aware than ever that I don't have one. Then last night Tony turns up with a new girlfriend and now I'm beginning to feel that I'm the only one without anyone and I'll never meet someone new.'

Mum put her hand on my arm and gave it a squeeze. 'A gorgeous girl like you – course you will.'

'No, I won't. I must be doing something to put boys off. What's wrong with me?'

'*Wrong* with you? Nothing.'

'Or maybe I shouldn't be so fussy. Maybe I'm aiming too high, for someone who doesn't exist. Maybe I should just go out with whoever's available?'

'Never,' said Mum. 'You just haven't met the right one yet. I remember when I was a teenager, I used to be quite stroppy and say exactly what I thought and that *definitely* seemed to frighten off the boys. A friend of mine said that I had to learn to compromise - that boys liked girls to be cute, like kittens, and that I'd have to learn to shut my mouth. Yuck, I thought. I could never be one of those whimpering girlie girls who don't know their own mind. But there were times when I doubted myself and thought, what's wrong with me? I thought I'd never meet the right boy or one who I could be myself with. It was rubbish. When you meet the right boy, he likes you exactly the way you are and you don't have to put on any act. You hold out until it really feels right. For *you* and not your friends or anyone else.'

'So how do you know if it's right?'

'You just do. You can't stop thinking about him. You're happy around him. But mainly because you can be yourself with him. More yourself than with anyone.'

I nodded. I knew what she meant. I felt like that when I was with Tony.

'I'm off now,' said Mum, getting up. 'You have a lie-in, you lucky thing. Holidays. I *wish*. And Dad told me to tell you that the offer's still open for you to go with him next weekend to that workshop if you want. You never know, you might enjoy it.'

I shook my head. 'No thanks.' Being stuck with a load of adults straining to contort themselves into yoga postures wasn't my idea of fun. 'But thanks for the tea and sympathy, Mum.'

'Any time.' Mum smiled, then began singing as she

went out the door. 'Some day Lucy's prince will come.'

'Mu-*um*,' I groaned. 'Let the whole house know, why don't you?' Honestly. She could be really lovely and sensitive one minute, then completely blow it the next.

Steve was slumped over a cup of tea at the kitchen table when I got downstairs.

'What's up with you?' I said, looking at his long face.

'TJ's off today,' he said. 'Scotland. She wants you to call her before she goes.'

Of course. She was going on holiday with her mum and dad. Poor Steve. He looked really down in the dumps about it.

'It's only for a week,' I said. 'You'll live.'

'Uh,' he said, then glanced up at me. 'You all right after last night?'

'Uh,' I answered, making an effort to speak his language.

That was as close as Steve and I ever got to a heart-to -heart. He's not very good at talking about his feelings, but maybe that's just because he's my brother and he's different with other people. Sometimes I wonder what he talks to TJ about. Or maybe he doesn't. Maybe she likes the silent types or men of few words, like 'uh' or 'nah'.

Lal, on the other hand, is different altogether. He's like Nesta – says what he thinks, asks what he wants to know.

A thumping on the stairs announced his arrival and he burst into the kitchen and helped himself to a large bowl of Shreddies.

'So, Lucy,' he said, sitting opposite me at the table. 'I heard you left Ben's party early last night. What was all that about?'

'And who are you?' I asked. 'The Spanish Inquisition?'

He took no notice. 'You and Tony? Or not you and Tony? Have you broken up? Gone off you, has he?'

Tactful as ever, my brother. 'We were never really *together* together,' I said. 'And no, he hasn't gone off me, he . . .'

'Want me to beat him up?'

I laughed. I knew he didn't mean it. 'Yeah. Like you could.'

'No one messes with my sister,' he said. 'Are you upset?'

'I'll live.'

'That means you are.'

'Leave off her,' said Steve.

'Boys are only after one thing,' said Lal. 'Did he finish with you because you wouldn't . . . you know . . . put out?'

'*Lal*,' said Steve. 'It's none of your business.'

'He never said anything about that,' I said, 'but it probably had something to do with it.'

'So put out,' said Lal. 'Then he'll have you back.'

'And when did you become the expert on relationships?' I asked.

63

Lal shrugged. 'Boys like girls who put out. Everyone knows that.'

I felt myself starting to get really miffed with him. 'And what about your treat-'em-mean-to-keep-'em-keen philosophy?' I asked. 'Last month that's what you told me. You can't follow two different sets of rules. I can't put out *and* treat 'em mean to keep 'em keen, can I? *Can* I?'

Lal looked confused for a moment.

'And since when did your angle win the girls?' I went on. 'I know you might have snogged a lot but how many of them have hung around to go out on proper dates? You've never even had a proper girlfriend, so you can't talk.'

'Don't want a committed girlfriend,' said Lal sulkily. 'Girls are nothing but trouble when you get to know them properly.'

'Not all boys are like Lal,' said Steve. '*Some* boys like girls for their company.'

'Who are you kidding?' asked Lal. 'I'm just being honest here.'

'So am I,' said Steve. 'I want to be with a girl who's got a good personality. Who I like being with. You just want to snog as many as you can so that you can boast to your mates about it.'

'And what's wrong with that? No, you take my advice, Lucy. Put out.'

'What? So that he can put me on his conquest chart?' I asked. 'There's more to relationships than scoring points, you know.'

Lal has a chart on the back of his door – The Snog Chart. He and his mate Harry are having a competition to see who can snog the most girls per week. When they get off with one, they come home and mark it on the chart. Like when Lal was at the party, they're not at all choosy about who they kiss or even if they like the girl, only that it's another conquest for the chart. Lal's winning by two this week.

'You should be more like me,' said Lal. 'Don't get hung up on one person and get your heart broken. Play the field. You need more experience. Snog loads of boys and boost your confidence.'

I'd had enough. 'I think I'll go and call TJ,' I said, getting up. 'Thanks so much for the advice, boys. I'm *so* lucky to have brothers like you. "Uh" from Steve and "put out" from you, Lal. Thanks, it's really helped.'

I couldn't believe it. Lal looked chuffed. Maybe he actually thought I *meant* it and was genuinely thanking him!

After I'd called TJ to wish her a happy holiday, Nesta rang to check I was OK after last night.

'I'm fine,' I assured her. 'It would be no biggie if all of you didn't keep going on about it. So first, I want you to stop trying to find boys for me. And second, don't worry.'

'So, don't you want to know about Tony?'

'Um, maybe.'

'He says he's tried your mobile a hundred times but you keep it switched off these days so he asked me to ask you to call him.'

'I've got nothing to say to him,' I said. 'Anyway he's got a new girlfriend now, so why does he want to speak to me?'

Part of me was hoping that she'd say because he realised that he'd made a terrible mistake and wanted to go out with me after all.

'He says he still wants to be friends,' said Nesta.

'And we all know what that means, don't we?'

'I guess,' said Nesta.

'So who is the blonde he was with?'

'Name's Georgia. He met her at the bowling alley.'

'Are they going out?'

Nesta was quiet for a few moments. 'Looks like it. I *am* sorry, Lucy.'

'Did you tell him I was there and left last night?'

'*No.* Course not. His ego's inflated enough as it is. Anyway, the other reason I rang is, do you want to come over?'

'Oh Nesta, not yet. I'm not ready to face him yet. Give me a few more days or call me when you know he's not going to be there.'

'OK, well, phone me later, OK?'

'Nesta, I'm fine. You don't have to check up on me every five minutes.'

'How about every hour, then?'

'Fine,' I said. 'But don't worry, I've got loads to do.'

I put the phone down and wondered, loads of what, exactly? It was only the first week of the holidays and I'm so desperate for stuff to do that even the thought of school seemed appealing. It wasn't meant to be like this, I thought, as I gazed out of the window.

Five minutes later, Izzie phoned.

'You'll never guess what,' she said.

'What?' I asked, fearing the worst. That she'd found some boy for me and was going to fix me up on a blind date.

'My mum saw this advertisement in your dad's shop. For a workshop in Devon. To get back to basics, aid relaxation and find balance in this hectic world, it says. Anyway, she wants to go. We're talking about *my* mum here, Lucy! My straighter-than-straight mum. She wants to go and chill out . . . Your dad's going, isn't he?'

'Yeah,' I said. 'It's run by a friend of his. He asked me to go, but I said no way.'

'But Mum's just booked for both of us, so I'm going to be there,' said Izzie. 'Oh please come as well. It'll be brilliant. We'll have a laugh if we both go.'

Suddenly, the idea had appeal. A few days hanging out with Izzie and no Ben and no boys. We wouldn't have to do all the classes. It could be fun.

'Well, I suppose . . .' I began.

'Excellent,' said Izzie. 'So that's settled then. Pack your things.

Chapter 7

Workshop
Weirdos

The workshop was being held at an old farmhouse manor on top of a hill near Bigbury in Devon. Dad and I drove down on Friday afternoon and Izzie and her mum arrived soon after. The view from the car park was stunning, and in the distance we could see the sea.

A pretty blonde lady in a pink tracksuit came out to meet us, swiftly followed by a boisterous black Labrador. He made a beeline for Mrs Foster as soon as she got out of her Jaguar and stuck his nose straight up her skirt.

'He's clearly in the Lal camp of thinking,' I giggled to Izzie as we watched her mum attempt to push the dog down with one hand and struggle with one of her many Louis Vuitton cases with the other.

'Sorry about Digby,' said the tracksuit lady, grabbing his collar and pulling him away. She put her hand out to Mrs Foster. 'Hi, I'm Chris Malloy and as you've gathered, this is my dog, Digby. He's still young and tends to get a bit overexcited when we have visitors.'

'She's not going to like it,' whispered Izzie as her mum gave Chris a tight smile. 'You know how she feels about dogs. All those hairs and muddy paws . . .'

I laughed. I knew *exactly* how she felt about dogs. I was never allowed to take ours into the house if ever I visited Izzie when I was out walking them. Mrs Foster has a thing about cleanliness. She's impeccable, her house is impeccable, her car is impeccable. Izzie always jokes that she doesn't use perfume, she uses disinfectant instead. This was going to be interesting, I thought, as I watched her totter on high heels round to the back of the car.

'How long does she think this workshop is going to last?' I asked as Izzie and I helped her unload the boot. She seemed to have brought enough luggage for three months.

'Oh, you know what Mum's like,' said Izzie. 'Has to have the right outfit for every occasion.'

'I don't think she'll be expected to dress for dinner in a place like this. More like tracksuits and T-shirts. And high heels in country lanes?'

'Try telling Mum that,' sighed Izzie, who like me, was wearing jeans and trainers. 'Anyone would think we're going to meet the Queen with the clothes she's brought down.'

Chris showed us around the farmhouse and where we were to sleep, and I could see at once that Mrs Foster didn't approve.

'I assumed that we all had our own private room,' she said, frowning as Chris showed us a whitewashed dormitory at the back of the house with bunk beds. 'I mean this *is* supposed to be a weekend of rest and relaxation.'

'We think it makes for a better atmosphere.' Chris smiled. 'Everyone gets to know each other really fast on a course like this. Soon you'll all be getting along like old friends.'

'And there's a yeti living in my fridge,' I whispered to Izzie as I glanced over at the other ladies who were busy unpacking their weekend cases. There were five of them: two old ladies with glasses and long grey hair who looked like sisters and were dressed in the sort of clothes my mum wears, i.e., charity shop cardigans and long hippie skirts; a younger woman with short spiky hair with pink streaks through it and a nose ring; a slim, blonde lady who was sitting on the end of her bed in a meditation pose with her eyes closed; and finally, a very plump lady with big teeth who was helping herself to a sandwich and a flask of tea. They glanced up at us when we walked in and the plump one gave us a wave.

'Hi, I'm Moira,' she said, then indicated the beds with

a sweep of her hand. 'You got any preferences about where you want to sleep?'

'As far away from here as possible,' whispered Mrs Foster, turning away. 'Izzie, I don't think I can do this.'

'Oh, come on, Mum, it'll be fun. Like a sleepover for adults.'

'Yes . . . fun,' said Mrs Foster, unconvinced.

Izzie and I bagged the bunk bed in the corner, leaving Mrs Foster to take the bunk above Moira. It was hysterical. Everyone stared at her as she unpacked and took over the whole wardrobe with her clothes. When that was full, she hung even more on the board at the end of her bed *and* the one at the end of our beds.

After half an hour, Chris popped her head round the door. 'When you've finished, we'll be serving herbal teas in the dining room, then we'll all get together for introductions and to go through the schedule.'

'Herbal tea?' said Mrs Foster, wrinkling her nose up. 'I'd kill for a decent cup of coffee after that drive.'

'Caffeine,' spat the slim, blonde lady. 'It raises the heart rate and *we've* come to relax.'

Moira winked at Mrs Foster. 'Hence the flask,' she whispered. 'Sometimes I have to have a proper cuppa. Anyone want an egg and cress sarnie?'

Poor Mrs Foster looked as though she'd landed in a prison camp.

'Come on, Mum, let's go and meet the others,' said Izzie, leading her out the door.

In the dining room, the men had already gathered and were sitting about sipping mugs of tea.

'Bit bare,' said Mrs Foster, glancing round at the brick walls, long pine tables and benches. 'When the ad said get back to basics, it really did mean it.'

'Oh ... my ... god ...' whispered Izzie, looking round at the men. 'Which one do you want?'

There were five men including Dad, who was chatting to Chris by a hatch to the kitchen. One of them was bald and very fat, and was sweating profusely in a lime green shell suit. Another had grey grizzly hair, trousers that were too short and open-toed sandals. The third man was wearing a T-shirt and a sarong, and had blond dreadlocks down his back. And the fourth was about six-foot-six, very skinny, and was dressed in Lycra cycling shorts to show off his very knobbly knees.

'I'll have one of the wrinklies,' I whispered back. 'You can have Mr Dreadlock, so that leaves Cycling Shorts for your mum.'

Mrs Foster overheard. 'Thanks a bunch,' she said, then giggled. 'And, ahem ... those shorts don't leave much to the imagination, do they?'

'*Mum*,' said Izzie in a stern voice. 'Be*have*.' But I could see that she was relieved that her mum was beginning to chill out a bit.

As we sat down to drink our camomile tea, Chris came over to join us. 'I know everyone's a bit older than you,' she said to Izzie and me, 'but my son Daniel will be here tomorrow. He's sixteen, so at least you'll have some company around your own age.'

'If he's anything like this lot, I can't wait to meet him. *Not*,' whispered Izzie when Chris had moved on to chat to some of the others. 'Wonder if he's an open-toed-sandal type or an anorak?'

'As long as he doesn't wear cycling shorts,' I joked. But I didn't really care. I was starting to enjoy myself even though the assorted guests looked like a bunch of weirdos and were all loads older than us. I didn't feel like I was Single here. I was just Lucy. And Izzie was just Izzie again, not Izzie and Ben.

After tea and rye biscuits that tasted like cardboard, Chris asked us all to sit in a circle and then threw a beach ball at my dad.

'OK,' said Chris. 'Whoever has the ball, say a little about yourself, why you're here and what you hope to get out of the weekend. When you've had your say, throw the ball on.'

Mrs Foster looked like she was going to throw up.

'I hope we don't all have to hug each other after this,' she whispered to Izzie.

'Hi. I'm Peter Lovering,' said Dad. 'I'm from London and I run a health shop. I'm here for the rest and relaxation.'

Everyone murmured their approval as Dad threw the ball at the slim blonde lady who'd been meditating in the bedroom.

'Hi, I'm Sylvia. I'm striving for a pure mind and body and I'm a colonic irrigation specialist.' More murmurs of approval, but I couldn't resist.

'That must be a crap job,' I whispered to Izzie, whose shoulders started to shake with suppressed laughter.

'I'm Moira and I've just got divorced so it's all been rather stressful for me of late . . . I do Swedish massage.'

'For when you need to be kneaded,' I said to Izzie.

'I'm Priscilla,' said one of the grey-haired ladies. 'I work as a gardener and I need to find myself.'

I didn't have to say anything this time as Izzie turned to me and coughed, 'Doesn't need to go far, then. She's right on that chair!'

'I'm Jonathan, but my friends call me Tabula,' said Dreadlocks. 'My third eye was recently opened on a trip to Goa. I need to close it again as I can't take the inner visions . . .'

I couldn't look at Izzie for fear of bursting out laughing.

'I'm Nigel,' said Cycling Shorts. 'I want to get some fresh air.'

'Shouldn't wear his shorts so tight, then,' was my comment this time.

'Hi, I'm Grace,' said Pink Highlights, 'and I work as a vegetarian cook and wanted some time out for me.'

She threw the ball to Izzie.

'I'm Izzie,' she said. 'I'm fourteen. I'm into astrology, crystals, feng shui, aromatherapy, self help. I've come with an open mind.' Murmurs of approval. 'Oh and I'm also into witchcraft.' After which the murmurs of approval turned to looks of concern, especially from her mother.

She threw the ball at her mum. 'I'm Laura Foster. I work in the financial sector in the City and, as my daughter keeps telling me,' she smiled at Izzie, 'I need to find some balance in my life.'

She threw the ball at me. 'I'm Lucy. Um . . .' I said, turning bright red. I couldn't say that I'd just come along for the ride and wanted an excuse to spend some time hanging out with my mate. 'Er, um, I . . . whatever. Open mind, see what happens. Yes . . . um, that's all.' I threw the ball at the second grey-haired lady but I must have thrown it harder than I intended, as it knocked her glasses off. 'Ohmigod, sorry, I'm sorry.' I leapt up. 'Are you all right?'

She adjusted her glasses and gave me a filthy look. 'I'm Prudence. I work in a school library and need to get away from all the noisy kids I have to deal with every day.'

Oops, I thought. Made a friend for life there, then.

Next was Hubert, the bearded man. He was an osteopath.

'I bet he knows how to have a cracking good time,' I said to Izzie.

Then Eric, the bald man, said he was there because his wife said she'd leave him if he didn't learn how to relax.

'Well, you've all come to the right place,' said Chris, getting up and handing out a sheet of paper to each of us.

'OK,' she said. 'Tonight we're not going to do much – just let you settle in and relax – then tomorrow, we start. The schedule is there on your paper, so take a quick look and do ask if there are any questions.'

I glanced at the paper.

6.00 a.m.: yoga salute to the sun and meditation.

'Six a.m.,' I said to Izzie. 'You mean there are *two* six o'clocks in a day?'

Izzie punched my arm. 'And you'll be up, if I have anything to do with it.'

'But the weekend's about relaxation. We ought to be having a lie-in.' I looked back at the paper.

7.00 a.m.: breakfast
8.00 a.m.: brisk group walk
10.00 a.m.: tea

I got as far as ten-thirty and I had to bite my tongue to stop myself from bursting out laughing. It said that there was to be a talk about overcoming dependency and leaning on things that weren't good for you, like cigarettes and alcohol. It was called Kick Your Crutch in Devon. Izzie had also seen it and I could see she was trying to contain herself as well. Her shoulders were heaving up and down as she continued down the schedule.

12.30 p.m.: lunch

2.00 p.m.: massage workshop

3.30 p.m.: tea

4.00 p.m.: group counselling session

6.00 p.m.: group visualisation

7.00 p.m.: supper

8.30 p.m.: 'cookery for calm' demonstration, then a relaxation game and wind down.

'I like the look of the lunch,' I said to Izzie.

'No. It's *all* going to be brilliant,' she said. 'Especially when we get to kick our crutch.'

That set us both off again and I had to leave the room pretending that I was having a coughing fit.

Chapter 8

Om Mani Padme Bum

Mrs Foster lasted one night.

While the rest of us were cross-legged in the meditation room the next morning, chanting '*om mani padme hum*', she was on her mobile, frantically trying to find the nearest five-star hotel with an en-suite bathroom. And Jacuzzi.

'I'm sorry,' said Izzie at breakfast. 'I think Prudence and Priscilla's synchronised snoring was the last straw. Then when Moira started breaking wind for Britain . . .'

'I know. Must have been last night's soya burgers and cabbage. But no biggie. At least you'll be here most of the time.'

Izzie looked sheepish. 'We're going straight after breakfast. She wants to make sure we have a decent room. I'll make her come back once we've checked in, though. Probably after lunch.'

And so Izzie and Mrs Foster disappeared down the lane leaving me to kick my crutch on my own.

We started with the walk, which was fine until Chris made us stop on the outskirts of the village to do stretch exercises. There were a bunch of local kids hanging about near a telephone box and they seemed to find the assorted weirdos straining to reach their toes highly amusing. I wanted the ground to give way and swallow me up.

After that, it was the talk about kicking your crutch. It was interesting in the end, but it wasn't half as much fun as it would have been if Izzie was there to sit at the back and giggle with. The lecturer talked about time management then gave all sorts of alternatives to having a gin and tonic and a cigarette after work or stuffing yourself with food when you feel miserable. I suppose chocolate and ice cream are my crutches when I'm low, but I reckon that if you don't overdo it, sometimes a crutch can help, especially if it's made of double pecan fudge.

After an uninspiring lunch of nut roast and lentils, there was still no sign of Izzie or her mum so I went back to the dorm and rang her on my mobile.

'When are you coming back?' I asked.

'Oh Lucy, I'm so sorry. Mum loves it here and I

have to say it is pretty cool. Huge beds, ginormous bathroom, comfy sofas everywhere with all the latest magazines. You'd love it – all the glossies, *Vogue*, *Tatler* and *Harpers* and . . .'

'Yes, but when are you coming back to the prison camp?'

'That's just it,' said Izzie. 'They have a beauty salon here and Mum's booked herself in for a pampering afternoon. She says this is more the kind of weekend she had in mind. Total indulgence and lying about being waited on. I am sorry. You know I'd love to be there with you, but she's booked me in for a manicure this afternoon.'

I looked around at our sparse dorm that now smelt of Moira's egg and cress sandwiches. I couldn't help wishing that Mrs Foster had taken me as well. In fact, I was beginning to wish I hadn't come at all, considering it was Izzie's idea in the first place.

'Look,' said Izzie reading my thoughts, 'you have to come and see this place. Why don't you skip the session after tea and come down here. It's not far. Just left of the village that you can see at the bottom of the hill. Ask for Montbury Lodge if you get lost. Big old hotel overlooking the bay.'

'Fantastic,' I said, my spirits starting to rise again. 'I'll be there.'

Maybe I could have tea and scones and Devonshire

clotted cream. Lie back on a big squashy sofa and read the new *Vogue*. The weekend was looking up after all.

I trooped along with all the others into the meditation room for the massage session, thinking that at least this should be enjoyable. Maybe not as luxurious as the hotel, but it would be a massage nonetheless.

After the teacher gave us a demonstration, we put mats out on the floor and I got paired with Prudence. It was my turn to massage first, so I held up the towel so that she could get undressed in privacy. She lay on the mat and I gave her a gentle massage. Nesta would have had a fit if she'd seen her, I thought, as I rubbed her legs. She hadn't shaved or waxed in years and her calves were as hairy as a man's.

Then it was her turn to do me. I lay on the mat and closed my eyes, ready for a nice relaxing massage. Unfortunately, however, Prudence clearly saw it as a way to get revenge for me knocking her glasses off last night. Or maybe even revenge on all the kids that had ever annoyed her in the library. She was of the builder's school of massage. Slap, whack, hammer, as hard as she could.

This is *not* my idea of fun, I thought, as I lay there with my neck twisted to one side while some mad woman with hairy armpits used me as a way to vent her anger.

Dad didn't seem to be enjoying it much either, as he had the bald man massaging him and he appeared to have studied at the same massage school as Prudence.

It seemed that everyone had taken great care to make sure that not too much flesh was exposed and that they were warm and covered in towels. Except Cycling Shorts, that is. He seemed to have no inhibitions at all and was walking about in a pair of faded blue Y-fronts. I quickly closed my eyes and couldn't help but think once again what a laugh we'd have had if Izzie had been there. As Prudence yanked my leg out of my hip, I twisted my neck the other way and looked at my watch. Twenty minutes to go. Argh argh *arrghhh*.

Dad had no objection to my opting out of the group counselling session when I told him I wanted to go to find Izzie.

'I guess you get enough psycho babble round the kitchen table at home, so fine, go,' he said. 'In fact, I'll give you a lift down there.'

When we got down to the village, we asked where the hotel was and he dropped me in a small square in front of a drive lined with rhododendron bushes that led up to the hotel.

'There it is,' he said, pointing at a gate with a brass sign that said 'Montbury Lodge'. 'Can you make your own way back or ask Mrs Foster to drop you? Any problems, call me on your mobile. I . . . um . . . have a few things I have to do before I go back.'

As I made my way up to the hotel, I turned back to wave him off, but he'd already parked the car and was heading with a determined walk to a building on the left of the square. I had to laugh when I saw what it was. The King's Arms, the local pub.

I felt slightly intimidated as I went into the reception of the hotel as it looked so grand. Then I remembered what Nesta always told me when I felt like this - that people can only ever make you feel inferior if you give them permission. I belong here as much as anyone, I thought, as I pulled myself up to my full four-foot-nine. I approached the desk and pressed the bell. I looked around at the enormous marble fireplace, deep sofas, polished furniture and huge vases of fresh lilies every-where. A few guests were sitting in a bay window in reception and helping themselves to a cream tea. Excellent, I thought, in anticipation of the one I'd be having in about fifteen minutes.

'Can I help you?' asked a lady with glasses appearing behind the desk.

'Yes, I'm here for Mrs Foster and her daughter,' I said.

'You just missed them,' said the lady. 'They went out about fifteen minutes ago. Would you like to leave a message?'

'Um, no thanks,' I said and made my way out and down the long drive again.

Why hadn't she phoned me? I wondered, as I reached the gates and rooted round in my bag for my mobile. I couldn't find it and realised that I must have left it back in the dorm when I'd called Izzie earlier. I looked to see if Dad's car was still there and saw that he had just got in it and was about to drive away. I darted out of the gate and smack, I crashed right into someone who was walking past talking to someone on a mobile. His phone went flying out of his hand and landed on the pavement.

'*Oi!* Watch where you're going,' he cried as he bent down to pick up the phone.

'Oh, sorry,' I said. 'I'm so sorry. Are you OK?'

'I am, but I'm not sure that my phone is,' said the boy, pressing a few keys and putting the mobile to his ear.

'I, er, didn't mean to . . .' I said as I saw Dad driving away in the distance. 'I was . . .'

'Yeah, you were daydreaming.'

'I was trying to catch my dad, actually,' I said. Then he turned to face me properly and I had to catch my breath. He was *cute*. Actually more than cute, *très* handsome. Blond, with very blue eyes and cheekbones to die for. 'Is your phone OK?'

He dialled a number and began to walk away. 'Yeah. No thanks to you.'

Probably the local village heart-throb, I thought. Probably got a million girls after him. Not this one, though. I made a face at his back. I don't like boys who can't at least make an effort to be nice, no matter how good-looking they are.

Your village phoned. They want their idiot back.

Chapter 9

Big
Brother

There were three messages on my mobile from Izzie when I got back to the dorm.

'Mum's bumped into a friend from the City,' said the first one. 'She was having a facial in the hotel salon. Anyway, she's got a second home down here and has insisted that we go for dinner. So don't come down today. Ring me to let me know you got the message.'

'Where are you?' said the second. 'Mum says you can come as well, so call me. We're leaving in about half an hour.'

'We're on our way,' said the third. 'I hope you got the messages. Call me as soon as you get this.'

I phoned her straight away and explained that I'd

been down to the hotel and missed her.

'Oh, I'm so sorry, Lucy. I feel awful, especially as I talked you into doing this course in the first place. Look, Mum's going out with her friend Kay tomorrow and I don't want to hang out with them so I'll be up first thing to spend the day up there. You OK?'

'Yeah,' I said. 'I'll survive. It's group visualisation tonight then wind down or something.'

'Sounds fab. I love doing visualisations. I wish I was there.'

'And *I* wish I was *there*,' I said and told her all about the day's events and classes. 'It would have been a hoot if you'd been here.'

'I know,' she said. 'I feel rotten about leaving you there. But I'll make it up to you in the morning. OK?'

'OK.'

After the phone call, I went along to the meditation room where the others were already lying on the floor on mats. Chris had put a few candles about and lit some joss sticks and in the background there was some soft new age music playing. The room was cosy and warm and the mats looked very inviting. This I can do, I thought, as I crept in, lay down by the door and closed my eyes.

Chris's soft voice began to lead us through the visualisation. 'Feel yourself getting drowsy, safe and relaxed.

Your body is feeling heavy, your limbs feel limp and warm. The only sensation you are aware of is your breath, rising and falling like gentle waves on a shore. You feel at peace, relaxed, warm, heavy . . .'

I was asleep in seconds. Next thing I knew, the lights were being turned up and the session was over.

'That was brilliant,' said Sylvia. 'I went somewhere really lovely. A garden and the sea . . . How was it for you, Lucy?'

'Um, yes, very relaxing,' I said, rubbing my eyes. I didn't feel too bad, though, as it looked like I wasn't the only one who had nodded off. Half of the guests were still comatose on the floor, Moira was dribbling onto her mat and Prudence and Priscilla were doing their synchronised snoring again. As everyone began to get up and shuffle off to the dorms, I became aware of a figure on a mat at the front of the room. He hadn't been there in the day and he was sitting with his back to me. Oh, must be Chris's son, I thought, as I got up to leave. Then he turned and looked up. My jaw dropped when I saw who it was. The boy from the village whose phone I'd knocked flying.

'You,' he said, getting up and coming over to me.

'*You*,' I said.

'Daniel, this is Lucy, Lucy, this is Daniel,' said Chris, joining us.

'Yeah,' said Daniel, looking really disinterested, 'we met

already. Or rather we *bumped* into each other in the village.'

I went bright red and made a beeline for the door. Dad followed me out and caught up with me in the hall.

'That wasn't very friendly,' he said. 'Where are your manners?'

'Where are *his*, more like,' I said. 'I accidentally bumped into him in the village and when I apologised, he was really offhand.'

'Come on, Lucy,' said Dad. 'This isn't like you. You have to make some effort.'

'Right,' I said, thinking, no way I'm making an effort with him, not until he learns to accept an apology with grace.

I went back to the dorm where it appeared that romance was in the air. Grace, Priscilla and Moira were all sitting on Moira's bunk giggling like schoolgirls. Apparently, Grace had taken a shine to Jonathan or Tabula, as he liked to call himself. Moira had swopped numbers with Cycling Shorts and Priscilla had a date with Hubert the osteopath.

'Where's Sylvia?' I asked, thinking that maybe I could have a chat with her or a game of backgammon or something.

'Gone back to London to look after a friend who was having a healing crisis,' said Prudence from her bunk, where she was eavesdropping on the others' conversation while pretending to read. She looked put out that Priscilla had got a date and she hadn't.

So it's me and you, pal, I thought. The singletons. I felt lonely there without Izzie to talk to and wondered whether to go over and try to be friendly to Prudence. But she was definitely in a sulk. She put earplugs in and began to read a book. This is like being on *Big Brother*, I thought, and you, dear Prudence, would be the first to be voted off.

In the end, I decided to get an early night. It had been a long day and we had another six a.m. start the next morning.

Izzie was true to her word and turned up straight after breakfast on Sunday. She was flushed with excitement as she slid in beside me at the breakfast table.

'Lucy, I've just met Daniel. Have you seen him? He's drop dead gorgeous. And so sweet. We must find out if he's single for you.'

'Oh Izzie, give me a break. I thought we'd left all that "Let's pair Lucy off" nonsense back in London. I *have* met him and I don't like him.'

At that moment, the dining room door opened and Daniel came in. He moved among the guests, chatting, smiling and fetching them whatever they wanted from the breakfast hatch.

'What's not to like?' asked Izzie, as she watched him move round the room. 'He seems really friendly and he dresses nicely.'

I glanced over at him. He did look cool in his black jeans and black T-shirt. He helped himself to a bowl of muesli, then came over to the end of the table where we were sitting.

'Hi,' he said, smiling at both of us. 'Anything I can get you?'

I shook my head.

'I've already eaten, thanks,' said Izzie. 'But please, sit with us.'

I made a mental note to kill her later.

He looked over at me. 'I guess we got off on the wrong foot yesterday, didn't we?' Then he grinned. 'Or at least *you* did.'

Oh, here he goes again, I thought. 'I *said* I was sorry.'

'I know. And the phone's fine. So let's pretend it never happened and start again. So, hi, I'm Daniel. And my mum runs this course for escaped lunatics.'

Izzie burst out laughing and I glanced up and looked at him properly. He was very good-looking and he had made an effort to be friendly. Maybe I should give him another chance.

'And I'm Lucy Lovering,' I said. 'I'm here with my dad.'

'How are you finding the weekend?'

'Um . . .'

Daniel grinned, then whispered. 'Slow torture?'

'It's more Izzie's thing,' I said diplomatically. 'Though I did enjoy the visualisation last night.'

'So did I,' he said. 'Great excuse to have a kip. And did you hear all that snoring?'

I was beginning to warm to him.

'So what are you into?' he asked.

'Oh . . .'

'Fashion,' said Izzie. 'Lucy's a fantastic designer. She makes loads of her own stuff.'

'You're kidding,' said Daniel. 'That's what *I* want to do when I leave school. I want to go to the London School of Fashion, then go and work in Milan or Paris.'

'Really?' I asked.

After that, we were off. We discovered that we had loads in common and like me, he knows all the famous designers and places to get offcuts of fabric, and often goes down to Portobello to trawl round the vintage clothes shops.

I decided to test his sense of humour and told him my latest favourite joke. 'A man is driving down a country road,' I said, 'when he spots a farmer standing in the middle of a huge field of grass. He pulls the car over to the side of the road and notices that the farmer is just standing there, doing nothing, looking at nothing. The man gets out of the car, walks all the way out to the farmer and asks him, "Excuse me, mister, but what are you doing?" The farmer replies, "I'm trying to win a Nobel Prize." "How?" asks the man, puzzled. "Well, I heard they give the Nobel Prize . . . to people who are out standing in their field." '

He cracked up laughing. 'OK, I've got one for you,' he said.

'What do you call a French man wearing sandals?'

'Dunno,' I said.

'Philippe Philope.'

I went down my wish list mentally. Sense of humour? Tick. Into fashion? Tick.

Izzie sat watching us with a sly smile, like she was a satisfied mother whose children were playing happily together.

Chapter 10

Shiatsu
Shmiatsu

Izzie was the first to point it out.

'He's *exactly* the boy on your wish list,' she whispered as we sat at the back of an aromatherapy demonstration in the morning. 'He's gorgeous, medium build, fit-looking, sense of humour.'

'But he may have a girlfriend, for all we know,' I said, taking one of the bottles of oils that was being passed round and inhaling deeply.

Izzie grinned. 'He hasn't. I asked him when you went to get your fleece after breakfast.'

'*Izzie*,' I said. 'What will he think?'

'He likes you,' she said. 'He asked loads of questions about you. And he doesn't live far from us. His mum runs a clinic in Chalk Farm, so they're just down the road.'

'Really?' I glanced over at Daniel, who was sitting two rows in front. Could Izzie's wish list really have worked?

After the aromatherapy session, Chris taught us a Chinese form of self-massage called Do-In. It was hilarious, as the technique seemed to consist of us having to beat ourselves up. Sort of.

'Clench your hand into a fist,' said Chris, 'and with a loose wrist, tap along the top of your shoulder, the side of your neck and as far down your back as you can reach.'

We all did as we were told, tapping along our shoulders, then legs and arms and it did seem to wake us all up. Everyone appeared to be in a better mood afterwards and the atmosphere had lightened considerably since yesterday. Daniel kept catching my eye and making daft faces as though he was in agony every time he hit himself.

Next we did shiatsu massage on our faces. We learned various points to press on, along the temple, jaw line and the sinuses, and I started to feel really good.

'This is brilliant, isn't it?' said Izzie, prodding along her eyebrow line. She seemed to be enjoying it all immensely.

I nodded and looked over at Daniel. Maybe the workshop had something to offer after all.

★ ★ ★

Next on the schedule was reflexology and, as in the massage class the day before, Chris told us to pair off. Great, I thought, this time I'll be with Izzie instead of Heavy Hands. But Izzie saw Daniel glance over at me and she turned to Moira.

'How about I go with you?' she asked her, then called to Daniel. 'Hey Daniel, Lucy needs a partner.'

I went scarlet. Sometimes my friends have no shame.

Daniel came straight over. 'I'll do you first,' he said. 'Lie back and take your trainers off.'

I lay on the mat and went even redder as he slid my socks off and dusted my feet with talc.

He smiled as he held my feet in his hands. 'Little feet.'

'I know,' I said. 'I hate being so small sometimes. All my friends are really tall. I'm the midget.'

'Good things come in small packages,' he said, still smiling. 'Personally, I like small girls.'

Ohmigod! I thought, as I mentally ticked off another thing on the wish list – likes petite.

As he followed his mum's instructions, I closed my eyes and drifted off into seventh heaven. His touch was so different to Prudence's. He was gentle and firm at the same time. I must add this to my list, I thought. Boy who can do a good foot massage.

'You've done this before, haven't you?' I asked.

He nodded. 'Mum taught me. It's nice, isn't it?'

I nodded. 'Heaven.'

After twenty minutes, we swopped places and I was relieved to find that his feet were clean with neat toenails. It would have been such a disappointment if he'd had smelly feet like my brother Lal's. I began the massage and glanced at his face to make sure I wasn't pressing too hard. He was lying back with his eyes wide open, looking up at me. I blushed furiously as a bolt of electricity went straight through me.

'Close your eyes,' I said.

'Why?'

'You're making me nervous.'

'Good.' He smiled, but he did as I asked and closed his eyes for the rest of the session. This is a new one, I thought. It's strange, but massaging someone's feet can be as much fun as snogging. Hope Dad's not watching, I thought, as I quickly glanced over to where he was. Luckily he was busy massaging Prudence's feet and hadn't noticed his daughter flirting with feet only two metres away.

Izzie looked over at me from where she was being massaged by Moira. She made her eyes go cross-eyed and pulled a face. So it wasn't so much the massage, but the person doing it with you. I thought back to the session yesterday and thanked God he hadn't been there then. I think I would have died if I'd had to strip off and have him massage my back. Although, when I thought about it, it made my stomach go funny, but in a nice way.

By lunchtime, I was floating on air and I wasn't sure whether it was all the treatments or whether it was Daniel.

'I think I may be in love,' I said to Izzie as we tucked into a lentil cheese loaf.

'Thought so,' she said. 'I saw the way you two were looking at each other in that last session.'

'I know,' I said. 'I'm going to add, "can do foot massage" to my perfect boy list. A definite requisite from now on.'

I was looking forward to the afternoon session and hoped that it would be more nice treatments. Then I'd have another chance to pair off with Daniel.

I soon realised that wasn't to be.

'This afternoon, we're going to start with an exercise to vent your pent-up emotions,' said Chris.

But I feel great, I thought. I haven't got any, so this is going to be a waste of time for me.

'It's a way to release anger or frustration that you can't express,' continued Chris. 'The sorts of feelings that if held in, can gnaw away at your peace of mind. I believe that negativity is better *out* that in, so now is your chance to let it all out.'

'Cool,' said Izzie, giving me a meaningful look. 'Unfinished business.'

'You can't yell at your boss,' Chris said, then looked at Iz and me and grinned, 'or your teacher or headmistress, maybe. So I'd like you to pick a cushion from the pile in the corner, then project onto it whatever or whoever has made you angry in the past — a lover, a parent, a colleague, a neighbour, a friend or even God. As it is sometimes not appropriate to let your anger out at the person directly, this is a way to free yourself of it without any repercussions.'

'Excellent,' said Izzie, heading for the pile.

I reluctantly went to pick a cushion with the others. The idea seemed a bit mad to me.

'OK,' said Chris, 'now let rip. You can throw your cushion, kick it, stomp on it, whatever you feel. Let your inhibitions go.'

Izzie picked a red cushion and started laying into it with passion.

'Poor cushion,' I said. 'What's it done to you?'

'I'm imagining it's all the terrorists who have killed innocent people,' panted Izzie as she jumped up and down on it. 'It makes me so mad sometimes as I feel so helpless and *angry* that I can't do anything.'

Izzie's always thinking about the problems of the world.

'Who are you going to beat up?' she asked, stopping for a moment to catch her breath.

I looked at the cushions. 'Someone closer to home.' I grinned and picked a brown velvet one. The exact colour of Tony's eyes.

At first, everyone was a bit shy, then Moira started getting into it. Then Cycling Shorts joined in. Then Eric and Tabula and then *my dad!* After ten minutes, the place sounded like a madhouse. Everyone got stuck in. I quickly glanced round to see what Daniel was doing as I didn't want to look an idiot in front of him, but he was going for it like the rest of them. If you can't beat them, join them, I thought, and got down on my knees and pummelled my cushion. I felt stupid to start with, then I began to get into it. That's for dumping me, I thought, as I whacked the cushion. And that's for turning up at that party with another girl . . . Whack! Thwump!

At the end of the session, I felt brilliant. Like a dam had burst. Everyone looked exhilarated, even Prudence, whose hair had escaped her bun and was sticking out all over the place. We should have done this session before the massage, I thought. It wouldn't have been so painful for me if she'd done this first. Chris was right. I hadn't known all those feelings were stuck inside. I felt much better about Tony. I knew that I'd be able to handle it if I saw him at Nesta's. We could, as he always wanted, be friends.

'I'm so fed up,' said Izzie as we filed out of the room

when it was over. 'I've got to go back to the hotel for the evening and I'll miss the lecture. It's about Bach Flower Remedies and I'm really into those.'

'I'll tell you all about it,' I said as Daniel caught up with us.

'Maybe we could go for a walk before the lecture,' he said, and Izzie gave me the thumbs-up behind his back.

'Maybe after,' I said. 'But first I'm going to walk Iz back to her hotel.'

My feelings about Daniel might have done a complete turnaround, but that didn't mean I'd forgotten everything that Nesta had taught me. Don't be too available. Don't be too easy.

I got back from the village an hour later and after putting on a little make-up, went into the dining room. There was no sign of Daniel.

All through the lecture afterwards, I kept looking at the door, expecting him to come in. But he didn't. Now what? I thought as I tried to concentrate on the talk. Was he peeved because I'd gone down to the hotel with Iz? Maybe he wasn't as nice as I'd thought he was. All my newfound inner peace evaporated like thin air as I watched the door.

'The Bach Flower Remedies are good for correcting any emotional imbalance,' said Chris. 'A lot of disease is literally that – dis-*ease*.' Then she began reading a list of the remedies out and what they were good for. 'Agrimony for mental torture behind a carefree mask, chesnut for failure to learn from mistakes, impatiens for frustration, mustard for gloom, scleranthus for mood swings, white chestnut for mental arguments, wild oat for uncertainty.'

That's me, and that's me, I was thinking as she went down the list.

'You'll only need one or two of them,' she said when she'd finished. 'And they're on sale in the dining room.'

After the talk, Chris was surrounded by people asking about the remedies, so I didn't get a chance to ask her where Daniel was. I went and found Dad instead.

'Can I have next month's pocket money as I want to buy some remedies?' I asked.

'Sure,' he said. 'Which ones do you want?'

'*All* of them,' I said.

Home
Sweet Home

Dad wanted to leave at the crack of dawn the next day so that he'd be back in time to open the shop at nine-thirty. He dropped me off at home first and it felt wonderful to be back in the cosy clutter of our kitchen with only Steve and Lal at the breakfast table instead of a bunch of strangers. Mum had already left for work and Steve and Lal soon went off to play tennis, so apart from the dogs, I had the whole house to myself. It felt great to take a long, hot, foamy bath without a queue of people banging on the door. To make a decent cup of tea and toast and strawberry jam. As I wandered round the house, I felt that I was seeing everything in a new light. The telly in the living room I could sit in front of and watch whatever I liked. My lovely bedroom that I didn't have to share. My CD player. And there'd be no more getting up at six a.m. to contort myself into unnatural positions.

My bed was calling me, so I turned off my mobile, switched on the answering machine and climbed under the duvet for a few hours of divine uninterrupted sleep.

'How was the course?' asked Mum when she popped in at lunchtime.

'Interesting,' I said. 'Some of it was a bit boring, but some of it was brilliant.'

'What were the people like?'

'Mad. But actually by the end of it, they'd sort of grown on me. Even a grumpy old one called Prudence.' Prudence had given me a huge hug when I left, as though I was her dearest friend. 'It's fantastic to be home, though. It feels so quiet and comfortable and roomy and there's loads I can do here.'

Mum smiled. 'Did I ever tell you the story about the farmer who felt his house was overcrowded and went to see a wise man?'

I shook my head.

'I use it at work sometimes when I'm talking to people who are unhappy with their lot in life. Want to hear it?'

I nodded.

'A farmer was very unhappy with his home,' she started.

'He had a wife and two daughters and only one room. He went to a wise man and asked what he could do to improve the situation. The wise man told him to move in three dogs. So he did what he was told. The next day, the wise man told him to bring in the cow from the field and let it sleep with them. The farmer thought it was a bit strange, but again, did as he was told. The next day, the wise man told him to bring in the chickens. The next day, a few goats. By the end of the week, there was a whole farmyard living in the house and it was unbearable. The farmer went back to the wise man and asked him what to do next. First take out the dogs then the cow, said the wiseman. Then the next day, the goats, then the hens. The farmer did what he was told until he was back to the original situation. His wife and his two daughters and himself. He was over the moon. It felt so quiet and spacious and the farmer never felt unhappy again.'

'Exactly,' I said.

'Well, let's see how long the feeling lasts,' Mum laughed. 'And your dad called me from the shop. He said that Chris's son was at the course?'

'Yeah, Daniel. Creep.'

'Why?'

'We were getting on brilliantly but then he just left, no message, nothing. Honestly, boys – you never know where you are with them.'

Mum smiled. 'Oh, I think you may hear from him sooner than you think. He phoned the shop today to ask for our number here.'

'Really?' I felt my spirits lift in an instant and dashed to check the answering machine. There were two messages flashing.

'Hi, it's Nesta, call me when you get back,' said the first.

'Hey Lucy, it's Daniel,' said the second. 'Sorry I had to leave last night, I hope Mum gave you the message and told you what happened . . . Anyway, I'll call again later.'

Luckily I didn't have to wait long as the phone went soon after Mum had returned to work.

'Hey,' he said.

'What happened?' I asked. 'I never got any message from your mum, but then we did leave first thing this morning so I didn't see her.'

'Flood,' said Daniel. 'Our neighbour phoned to say that a pipe had burst in his flat and was pouring water into ours. We're on the ground floor. Anyway, Eric was coming up to London at supper time so I cadged a lift. All sorted now, but I think I got here just in time. You must have been mad at me disappearing like that.'

'No, not at all,' I fibbed. 'I had a fabulous evening. To tell you the truth, I didn't realise that you'd gone until after the lecture.'

'Oh,' he said, sounding a bit disappointed. 'I was hoping

you'd missed me. I missed you. I felt like we really connected down there and I'd like to see you again, if that's OK with you.'

I grinned to myself. I loved the way he came straight out with it. No games, no pretending to be cool. We'd connected, and he wanted to see me again. I decided to be just as honest back.

'I'd like to see you again too. I really liked meeting you.'

'I've got a few things to do this afternoon. How about this evening?'

'Fab,' I said.

Life couldn't get better, I thought, after I'd put down the phone. I felt like I was floating on air. I was home. I had a date with Daniel. And there were weeks of the holidays left.

Chapter 12

Truly,
Madly, Deeply

The following Friday, I met Izzie and Nesta in Ruby in the Dust.

'At last,' said Izzie when I walked into the café. 'We were going to put out a missing person's alert.'

I grinned back at her. 'Not missing, just been out a lot.' I felt chuffed to be the one who'd been too busy to catch up, for a change.

'So, how's it going with dreamboy?' she asked as we took our favourite sofas in the window.

'Fantastic,' I said. 'I'm in *lurve* . . . Truly, madly, deeply.'

'What is this thing called love?' said Izzie.

'What? Is this thing called *love*?' I replied, joining in

one of our games – seeing how many different ways you can say the same sentence.

'What is this thing called, luv?' said Nesta.

'What is this *thing* called love?' I said.

'But it's great,' said Nesta, spooning the froth from her hot chocolate into her mouth. 'You deserve a decent boyfriend after my horrible brother.'

I'd had an amazing week with Daniel. We'd seen each other every day and decided to be like tourists in London. We went to the IMAX cinema in Waterloo, up on the London Eye, to the Victoria and Albert museum in Kensington to look at the costumes, to a photography exhibition at the Portrait Gallery and we spent ages cruising all the boutiques in Bond Street and Knightsbridge. He knew so much about fashion and its history, and I felt I was learning loads from him as well as having a good time. The best thing, though, was that I felt safe with Daniel. Secure. He phoned when he said he would, he was never late and he didn't play games about where I stood with him.

'He's as different to Tony as anyone ever could be,' I said. 'He's *so* romantic. And when I'm not with him, he sends me lovely text messages. Every day, sometimes five a day. Then on Wednesday when we were in Covent Garden, he bought me a rose and a little fluffy teddy bear. He said it reminded him of me.'

'Aw, sweet,' said Izzie. 'I wish Ben would do stuff like that. Knowing him, he'd probably say that kind of thing is all a commercial rip-off and the only people that benefit are the companies that make them for nothing.'

'That's what Steve says about Valentine's Day,' I said. 'But I think it's mainly because he never gets anything. I bet he'll feel differently next year if TJ sends him something.'

Nesta looked sad. 'Simon used to be all romantic with me when we first met, but lately, I don't know, it's like he's cooling off or something.'

'No, he adores you,' said Izzie.

Nesta shook her head. 'Nah, I know the signs. Like I phoned him yesterday and he hasn't called back yet. In the beginning, he always called me straight back.'

'I don't need to call Daniel,' I said. 'He always calls exactly when he says he will and sometimes even before. It's so fantastic not having to worry or wonder. You know, does he like me? Does he feel the same? I know he does.'

I was about to launch into telling them about what a great kisser he was, but Nesta looked downcast and I thought that maybe I was being a bit insensitive.

'You're probably imagining it,' I said. 'No one in their right mind would go off you.'

'Well, I only saw him once last week,' said Nesta, then pouted. 'It's been awful and every time I called to talk to you, you were out with Daniel. And even *you* didn't return my calls.'

'Don't be rotten, Nesta,' said Izzie. 'I bet that Lucy felt like that enough times when we were off with Ben and Simon, didn't you, Luce?'

'All in the past,' I said. All those times when I felt I was billy loner were ancient history. I was so happy now. I felt bowled over by Daniel's attention and the fact that someone wanted to be with me so much.

'I've never been dumped before . . .' Nesta started.

'Just because he hasn't returned one call doesn't mean he's going to dump you,' I said. 'He's probably been busy.'

'Too busy to talk to me? To return *one* call? Get real. There's one thing I *do* know about and that's boys. And when boys want to be with you, you don't have to spend time agonising over whether he will or won't call. If he wants to, he calls. What shall I do? Finish with him before he finishes with me? What?'

'Just play it cool for a while,' said Izzie.

'I *have*. I only called twice, then I thought, no way I'm doing this. Reject is not a role I want to play.'

I didn't know what to say. Usually it's me going to Nesta for advice not the other way around. But she did look fed up.

'It will be OK,' I said, remembering something I'd heard my mum say on the phone to one of her clients.

'All relationships go through down patches. It's probably just a phase and next week he'll be back banging on your door begging to see you.'

'Yeah,' said Nesta, making an attempt to brighten up. 'Sorry I'm being a downer. So, when am I going to meet loverboy?'

'Tomorrow, if you like. We're going to Notting Hill. We're going to go down to Portobello Market to look at the vintage clothes stalls. Do you want to come?'

'Yeah,' said Nesta, cheering up immediately. 'When the going gets tough, the tough go shopping. Anyway, I love it down there. What are you doing, Iz? Are you seeing Ben?'

Izzie shook her head. 'Nah. Actually, I need some space from him. All we ever do is band stuff. I've been locked up in his garage all week. An afternoon with the girls sounds great. Shall we call TJ?'

'No, I spoke to her,' I said. 'She's on her way back from Scotland and is going round to ours tomorrow to have the great reunion with Steve. Honestly, he's been like a limp lettuce while she's been away.'

'Right,' said Izzie. 'Tomorrow. That's settled then.'

Daniel was waiting for me outside Ladbroke Grove tube and at first he looked disappointed when he saw that I'd brought the girls. Sweet, I thought. He wants me all to himself. He was all in black and looking gorgeous as usual. I felt proud to introduce him to Nesta as *my* boyfriend.

'So, Lucy tells us that you want to do fashion when you leave school,' she said as we made our way to the market.

Daniel nodded and glanced at himself in a mirror in a window. 'I've started already, actually. I did some designs for our end-of-year fashion show at school. Got first prize and the local paper came and did an article.'

'Really,' said Nesta. 'We'd love to see them some time, wouldn't we?' She turned to Izzie, then back to Daniel. 'Has Lucy shown you hers?'

But Daniel wasn't listening. He'd seen a shop with an interesting display and had taken my hand and hauled me off. 'Sorry. Just *got* to show Lucy these designs,' he called over his shoulder.

When we got to the market, Daniel insisted that he buy us all a drink and took us to a café he knew. He asked the girls what they wanted, then went to order.

'He didn't ask if you wanted anything,' said Izzie.

I blushed. 'Oh, I trust his choice. He knows so much about everything, even coffee.'

Daniel came back a moment later with Cokes for Izzie and Nesta and double espressos for me and him.

'But you don't like espresso,' said Izzie as I took a sip.

'It's what everyone drinks in Milan. It's an acquired taste,' said Daniel. 'She'll get used to it.'

I might have been imagining, but I was pretty sure Izzie shot Nesta a 'look'.

As the afternoon went on, I could see that Nesta was feeling more and more miserable. She kept checking her mobile for messages and I don't think it helped that Daniel kept putting his arm around me and playing with my hair and kissing me at every opportunity. That's one of the things I like about him, it's like he's really proud to be with me.

After about an hour of Daniel and I running into shops and Daniel explaining to me why he thought this outfit worked and that one didn't, Nesta pulled me to one side. 'Izzie and I are going for a wander on our own. We feel that we're a bit in the way, so see you at the tube about four?'

'Yeah, cool,' I said. I didn't mind. It meant I had Daniel to myself again.

Daniel walked me to the tube when it was time and gave me a really smoochy snog in front of the girls before letting me go.

As I watched him walk away, he kept turning back and waving until he'd disappeared round a corner. A moment later, my mobile bleeped that I had a text message. 'Big hugs, little bear.'

I showed it to the girls. 'See what I mean? He's *so* sweet.'

This time Nesta gave Izzie the funny look.

They've been talking about me, I thought. You don't hang around with mates as much as I do and not learn to pick up when stuff's not being said.

'OK, so what's with the secret looks?' I asked as we went to buy our tickets.

'Nothing,' said Nesta unconvincingly.

'What do you think of Daniel?'

'Um . . . He's very good-looking,' said Izzie. I knew Izzie well enough to know that she was being diplomatic.

'OK, spill,' I said. 'What have you been saying about us?'

'Well he is a bit all over you,' blurted Nesta.

'*Nesta*,' said Izzie. 'They're in love.'

'So, didn't you like him?' I asked.

'It's not that I didn't like him,' squirmed Nesta, 'it's just, well, I thought he was a bit arrogant. And a bit self-obsessed. He talked about himself all afternoon and never once asked anything about Izzie or me. And I lost count of the number of times he checked his appearance in a window.'

Trust Nesta to say exactly what she thought. She can never hide her true feelings and sometimes it can sting.

'*Nesta*,' warned Izzie.

'Yeah, well, we could have been invisible for all he cared.'

Ah, I thought, not being the centre of attention is a new one for her. And she's clearly jealous because I have a boyfriend who's really into me and hers is cooling off.

'Well, I like him,' I said. 'And it's what I think that's important. It's me that's spending time with him. He's really great, you just need to get to know him better. He's not like anyone I've ever met before. Um . . . *you* like him, don't you, Izzie?'

She shifted awkwardly. 'He seems a bit different to when we were in Devon. But then so are you. You let him monopolise the whole afternoon, like that espresso – you *hate* strong coffee. And you went where he wanted and it was like, well, he was the only expert on fashion. Usually you have so much to say about it all and your designs are awesome. You were as quiet as a mouse all afternoon.'

'I talk to him a lot. I *do*. And I *like* listening to him. I feel like he knows so much more than me. I'm really learning from him,' I said.

'Just don't let him take you over,' said Nesta. 'Girls are either goddesses or doormats. Don't let him walk all over you.'

'I *don't*,' I said. 'How can you say that?'

Izzie looked awkward again. 'Nesta may have a point, Lucy.'

'Why? What do you mean?'

'It's about Daniel,' she said.

'What?'

'You might not like it.'

'Oh, just *tell* me, Izzie.'

'Well, remember Mark in the band? Ben's mate?'

I nodded. I'd met him at Ben's birthday.

'Well, he brought his girlfriend Amy along to rehearsal last night and she overheard me saying something about the weekend we had down in Devon. Anyway, she asked if I knew Daniel. I said, yes, my friend's going out with him . . .' Izzie looked at me anxiously.

'And?'

'Well, she said poor you. Apparently she went out with him last year and said he was a real pain. She said it all started out well, then it all got too much. He followed her everywhere, started telling her who she could and couldn't see . . .'

I was determined to stand up for Daniel. 'Well, actually, I already know about her. But he told me that *she* was the pain, always running off to her friends the minute they beckoned.'

'Well, she said to tell you to be careful and not to let him take over,' continued Izzie. 'She said he gets jealous if you even look at another boy. I hope you don't mind me telling you.'

I shrugged. 'No, course not. Anyway, she's an ex. Maybe she wasn't the right one for him. And besides, when does anyone ever have anything good to say about an ex-boyfriend? Maybe he dumped her and it's sour grapes.'

'Yeah, that's probably it,' said Izzie quickly. 'It's whether you like him that counts.'

'Exactly,' I said with a quick glance at Nesta, who had kept very quiet for once.

'Um, yeah,' said Nesta. 'Sour grapes. You like him. That's what counts.'

The tube journey home felt flat as we all sat lost in our own thoughts. It's not fair, I thought. I felt really hurt that they couldn't be happy that I'd met someone who really liked me. It was true that we always went where Daniel said, though. Was it possible I was turning into a mouse or a doormat around him? We *did* always talk about *his* designs and he still hadn't asked about mine. He was making the rules. But that was OK, I decided. It was my choice to go along with it and I'm not going to let what Izzie and Nesta think ruin it all.

Chapter 13

Goddesses

Things didn't improve much with Izzie and Nesta the following week, and it felt like an invisible wall had gone up between us. I spoke to them as usual on the phone but we talked about other things – what was on telly, what was happening at home . . . everything except boy stuff. Izzie invited me and Daniel to go to watch her band rehearse, but Daniel said it was his idea of a nightmare, so I didn't want to force him. People are different, I told myself, with different interests. You can't make everyone like everything the same and we did have a good time on our own, hanging out and exploring London again, even if it was him who chose where we were going every day. It felt like I was having a proper grown-up relationship.

However, despite everything I told myself about it not mattering what the girls thought, a seed of doubt had been planted in the back of my mind. Part of me wondered if I was letting him take over and giving in to him too easily.

Thank God for TJ. She came over to see Steve one evening and came into my room for a catch up.

'But I think he sounds great,' she said after I'd filled her in on the latest. 'You don't want some wimp who doesn't know what he wants or leaves it all up to you.'

'Nesta says I have to be a goddess and not a doormat,' I confided.

'Ah,' said TJ, 'but which goddess? There are loads of different types. There's Hestia, the goddess of the hearth, Athena, goddess of wisdom, Artemis, the huntress, Aphrodite the goddess of lurve and beauty . . . loads. What type of goddess do you want to be?'

Trust TJ to know a whole list of them, I thought. She has a different way of looking at everything. Like she sees all the shades of grey in between the black and white.

'I think Nesta meant I should be the one calling the shots and not him,' I said.

'I think it should be mutual,' said TJ. 'Like both of you decide. You do some things he wants and he does some things you want and you compromise on others.'

'Well, it's not that I didn't want to do all the things

we've been doing. We've had a great time.'

'Then there's no problem,' said TJ. 'But why not try picking some things you'd like to do next and see how he takes it. If he goes along with it, hey, no biggie.'

TJ was right. When she'd gone I had a think about what I'd like to do with him in the coming days. Bring him into my world, I decided. Invite him home and show him my designs. Maybe a walk in Golder's Hill park. I could show him all the lovely flower displays they always have there. Maybe see a movie at Hollywood Bowl. Introduce him to our favourite cafés. I made a list, then called him to see if he wanted to come up to Muswell Hill and meet in Ruby in the Dust on Thursday.

'Love to,' he said. 'I'll count the hours as I'm missing you already.'

Things were going to be fine.

'Bit of a dump, this,' he said, looking round as I bagged the best sofa in the window at Ruby's. The girls and I think it's a good spot because it feels private yet you can sit and watch the world go by outside.

'No it's not,' I said. 'It's got a lived-in feel. That's why we like it here.'

'We?'

'Well, actually it's Nesta's favourite.'

'And yours?'

'Um, mine? Er, I like loads of places, but we come here most.'

He shook his head. 'Sounds to me like you go along with your friends a lot.'

'No, not really . . .' I began to object.

'I'll take you somewhere with *real* style,' said Daniel, then looked at me softly and pulled me towards him. 'My little bear.'

I snuggled into his shoulder, but I wished he'd call me something else. The nickname was beginning to jar. Little bear, it sounded so yucky.

Then my mobile rang. I'd decided that I'd keep my phone on as even though Nesta had put a dampener on Daniel, she was still a mate and going through a bad time. I got up and went to the ladies to take the call.

'Who was that?' he asked when I came back to sit down.

'Nesta,' I said.

'What did she want?'

'We're all meeting up tomorrow,' I said. Nesta had decided that she needed a consultation with Mystic Iz for a tarot card reading about Simon. Of course I wasn't going to miss that, plus I was interested to know what the cards said about Daniel and me. I didn't tell Daniel that, as some boys are a bit sniffy about fortune-telling.

'But I wanted to take you to see a movie,' said Daniel.

'I am sorry. But, well, Nesta's having a bit of . . . er,

boyfriend trouble, so . . .' I didn't want to go into detail, as I thought it might be a bit disloyal to Nesta.

'You mustn't let your friends dump on you,' Daniel interrupted. 'The others will be there. Don't let her use you at her convenience. Like you're a dustbin for all her problems.'

'It's not like that,' I said, thinking he was being a bit unfair. I was beginning to get angry. He'd only met Nesta once. How could he possibly think she used me at her convenience? She was my mate and I felt that I ought to be there for her. Maybe his ex-girlfriend had been right. He had objected to her seeing her friends and now he was trying to stop me seeing mine. I was about to tell him how important my friends were when suddenly it occurred to me that he never talked about his friends. Maybe he didn't have any, with his attitude.

Then the phone went again. This time it was Izzie, phoning to check that I was going tomorrow.

'Can't you switch that off?' asked Daniel when I'd finished. 'You're with me now and you don't need friends calling you every minute.'

I decided not to be a doormat and stand my ground. 'These are my best friends, Daniel. I want to be there for them and I'd expect the same from them.'

I could see that he didn't like it and it didn't help that the phone went again five minutes later. This time it was

TJ checking in. Even though I took the call, I felt uncomfortable about it, as Daniel was starting to look bored. Maybe it *would* be easier to turn the phone off and pick up my messages when I got home.

'There, I've turned it off,' I said.

'Good girl,' said Daniel, putting his arm back around me. 'Now, where were we?'

After that, we chatted about our plans for the rest of the holidays and he seemed quite happy to do things that I wanted as well as things he wanted. So Nesta was wrong. He wasn't a total control freak, and I guess it *can* be a bit annoying when someone's mobile is going off every other minute.

As we sat sipping our drinks and gazing out the window, a stunning-looking boy with shoulder-length curly hair walked past. He was wearing a cool pair of sunglasses and looked Spanish.

'Now, he's got style,' I said.

'Why? Do you fancy him?'

'*No*,' I said. 'I was only saying I thought he looked good.' Last week, Daniel had commented on loads of girls and what they were wearing. It didn't mean anything.

Daniel snuggled up to me and nuzzled my neck. 'I don't want you looking at *anyone* except me,' he whispered.

Gerroff, said a voice in my head. I ignored it and took Daniel's hand. We were running out of holiday and I was determined to not let my inner arguments spoil our time together. Izzie says I have them because I'm a Gemini, the sign of the twins; hence the split personality. She's so right. Some days the twins get along just fine, but other times one of them is pre-menstrual and gets a bit stroppy.

But when I invited him to my house later that day, more cracks began to appear in my dreamboy. On opening the door, Ben and Jerry did their usual 'Oh my long lost friend' routine, leaping up with their tails wagging and trying to lick Daniel's face. I could see he didn't like it, so I had to take them away and shut them in the kitchen. They sloped under the table with their tails between their legs. As I closed the door, I glanced back at them and I swear Ben gave me the Nesta/Izzie disapproval 'look'. Like, 'Get rid of the killjoy, Lucy.' It didn't bode well.

I took him upstairs where I'd laid out my designs on the bed to be ready for him to look at. I'd even dressed the dummy that Mum had found for me in a second-hand shop. I thought it made my work look really professional.

'So, what do you think?' I asked as he picked up the outfits and studied them. I was really proud of some of them, particularly a couple of the tops I'd made from velvet trimmed with lace.

'Yeah, nice,' he said. 'Very nice. But . . . well, I can't see your voice coming through. You know, like a singer or a writer has a voice. It's the same with designers. Their clothes should make a statement and be instantly recognisable when you see them. Like me – as you know, I only do designs in black or white. And I only wear black. Yours are too varied not focused enough.'

'Oh,' I said, feeling gutted. I knew what he meant about designs having a voice or a signature, but I honestly thought that mine did. I always mixed old and new fabrics and my style was romantic but modern.

'You'll get there,' he said. 'These are very good for a beginner. Do you mind me being so honest? I feel that it's important in a relationship and I really want it to work with us. So no lies, no false praise.'

'No, no, I'm into honesty. I think it's very important,' I said, thinking, that it *was* one of the things that I'd written on my wish list, after all. But then I'd also written 'likes animals' and Daniel had made it very clear downstairs that he didn't. Or maybe it was because he didn't want the dogs' muddy paws ruining his clothes.

Daniel stood back and looked at me. 'OK then, since we're being honest, I think you should grow your hair longer. That urchin style is, well, a bit passé now.'

I felt hurt. I liked my hair short. So did everyone. Nesta said it suited my shape of face and made my cheekbones stand out. And no one's ever said anything negative about my designs. But I knew that part of learning is being able to take criticism, so I decided to be open-minded and listen to what he had to say. He had been doing it longer than me, after all.

He moved the clothes off the bed and slung them across the back of a chair. Then he chose a CD from my desk, put it in the player and sat back on my bed to flick through my latest copy of *Vogue*. I sat on the end of the bed and turned to look at him. I'm not sure if I like you anymore, I thought suddenly. Then another voice said, You're just sulking because he doesn't like your clothes. Then the other voice said, Well, I don't like his. Only black or white. How boring. *Arghh*, I thought. Here we go again with the arguing twins.

'What sign are you, Daniel?'

'Cancer.'

'That's the sign of the crab, isn't it?' I said, as a voice in my head said, Yes. Crab, crab, crabby.

Tarot
Readings

'And so gather the Witches of East Finchley,' I said as we all sat on the floor in Izzie's bedroom ready to do the tarot cards.

She did Nesta's reading first and it didn't look good, even to me, who doesn't know what they all mean.

'It says there's a bit of a stormy time in love coming up for you,' said Izzie, consulting the book, then pointing at a card with a picture of a pierced heart on it.

'Tell me about it,' groaned Nesta.

'I am doing,' teased Izzie. 'It doesn't necessarily mean bad, though. Just a difficult time. And the last card is the World, and that's always a good one. It means a goal is attained. Success.'

'Great,' said Nesta. 'Either way, I've decided to be positive. I mean, Simon's the longest I've ever been out with anyone and he is going to university in a couple of weeks. Maybe we do need to cool off a bit so that I can go out with loads of other boys and not feel like I'm cheating.'

My mum says that in life there are two types of people. Those who see a glass as half full and those who see a glass as half empty. Nesta's definitely a half-full type of girl.

TJ's cards were brilliant. Mostly cups, which the book said meant emotional happiness, then the Empress, which Izzie said meant a happy relationship.

'Excellent,' said TJ.

Izzie's reading was more complicated. 'I think it means that I'm unsure which way to turn,' she said as she looked at the layout, then studied her book.

'What did you ask about when you shuffled the cards?' I asked.

'Ben,' she said. 'It's time to call it a day, but you know, I don't want to hurt his feelings.'

'Why do you want to finish with him?' asked TJ.

Izzie shrugged. 'Dunno, really. I still really like him, but hey, you know, we're far too young to be tied down.'

'You sound like your mum,' I said.

'Heaven forbid I ever turn into my mother,' said Izzie. 'Please, God, no. It's just, all we ever do is band stuff or write lyrics. I do like doing that but not *all* the time. I want to have a bit of fun as well.'

I was dying to tell them about my last meeting with Daniel and ask them what they thought, but I already had a pretty good idea what Izzie and Nesta would say. Izzie would be all protective of me and want to phone him up and give him an earful for criticising me and Nesta would simply say, 'Dump him, life's too short.'

When they went downstairs to get snacks, I told TJ in private about the day before.

'You're right,' she said. 'You do have to accept criticism but only if it's constructive. Your designs are fabulous and you have a great eye for colour. There's room for everyone. I bet some of the most famous designers hate each other's designs, so it doesn't mean anything that he didn't like yours. Like, oh, I don't know their names but, say, that one who does bright colours?'

'Versace.'

'Yeah, him. I bet he doesn't like the subtle ones who do, you know, like simple classical stuff. What's his name? The one that does the aftershave?'

'Armani, and Versace is a she now. Gianni was shot outside his home a few years ago and so his sister took over the business.'

'See?' said TJ. 'You know loads about the fashion world. I bet he doesn't know that.'

'Everyone knows that, TJ.'

'Do they? Oh, sorry. I'm not the one to talk to about fashion, am I?'

'Goddesses, yes; fashion, maybe no.'

'But I do know that you have your own style and it suits you, Lucy. Remember when Nesta gave me that makeover and made me look like a Barbie doll. It wasn't me at all. It made me realise that you have to trust your own judgement about what suits you and not let others impose their ideas on you.'

I laughed. She was right. 'TJ, maybe you don't know the names, but I think that you know more than you realise.'

TJ looked at me with concern. 'I hope you don't mind me asking, Lucy, but . . . well, it's just, you do seem different since you met Daniel and I wondered if . . . are you having a good time?'

'Yeah. I mean, I know we had a bit of a glitch when I showed him my designs, but apart from that, we've done loads of things together. I feel like I've discovered London. We've been everywhere.'

'I know, but . . . you could do all that with anyone – with a teacher or your mum. I mean, do you have a good time, a laugh? Silly times and serious times when you really talk, you know, about what you want and all your plans? About how you feel?'

That made me think. We didn't really. He talked, or

rather, lectured. He liked an audience and I did find what he had to say interesting. But no, we didn't talk about personal stuff, not really, and we certainly never got silly. I couldn't imagine Daniel being silly. He's far too busy trying to be sophisticated, I told myself. But that's what I like about him. He's different.

'OK,' said Izzie, coming back in with a huge box of Liquorice Allsorts. 'Let's do Lucy's cards next.'

Nesta followed her in carrying a tray full of tortilla chips and Pringles and Diet Cokes.

Izzie handed me the cards and told me to shuffle them while thinking about my question.

What's going to happen with Daniel? I thought. What's going to happen with Daniel? Then I laid out the cards as Izzie told me.

'OK,' she started. 'Hmmm. The first card is the Page of Swords.' She flicked through her book then read what it said. 'This card denotes a young man with a strong will. He's very clever, but can be ruthless and unconcerned about the feelings of others.'

TJ gave me a knowing look. I guess that's true, I thought. He wasn't very sensitive when he looked at my designs.

'And it's crossing the Page of Wands. Another boy. Oh, that's interesting. Hmmm, some kind of conflict coming up, I'm afraid, as there's the Lovers card as well.'

'That's good, isn't it?' I said.

'It can be – let me just look it up,' said Izzie, turning to her book again. 'It says that you have a choice ahead of you, and the other cards are saying that you need to reassess.'

Just at that moment, my mobile rang. 'Daniel,' I said.

'Just checking in,' he said. 'What are you wearing?'

'Oh, jeans and a T-shirt. It's only us here.'

'Ah, but us designers, we're the ambassadors of style. Wherever we are, whatever we're doing.'

Oh, get a life said pre-menstrual twin in my head. Who does he think he is? The fashion police?

After that, we went downstairs to watch the *Pop Idol* video. Talk about taking criticism, I thought, as we watched some of the judges destroy people's performances. It was funny, though, especially a girl who sang 'YMCA' really out of tune. Then Daniel phoned *again*.

'I miss my little bear,' he said. 'What are you doing?'

'Watching *Pop Idol*,' I said.

'Oh, that rubbish.'

'It's not rubbish,' I said. 'It's great.'

'Well, you're obviously enjoying yourself, so I'll leave you to it,' he said huffily. 'When am I seeing you next?'

'I have to pick up some business cards for Mum in Hampstead tomorrow morning, so in the afternoon?'

'Great,' he said. 'We could go round Camden.'

'Fine,' I said. I wished he'd get off the phone so I could get back to having a laugh with the others as we watched the excruciating performances on the video.

'OK, going now. Miss you.'

'Yeah,' I said, then hung up. Whatever, I thought.

'He's really got it bad, hasn't he?' whispered TJ.

I nodded. The fact that he phoned so often was starting to bug me. I was beginning to feel suffocated. I decided that next time I saw him, I'd take the bull by the horns and have a word about maybe giving each other a bit more space. After all, Mum's always saying that you have to work on relationships and not give up at the first hiccup. It was still early days for Daniel and me, and maybe it was going to take time to adjust to each other.

Chapter 15

Page of Wands

The sun was shining with not a cloud in the sky the next day as I walked down Hampstead High Street. Everyone seemed to be enjoying the weather, dressed in light cottons and sitting about outside the cafés. I went and picked up Mum's cards from Rymans and decided to have a mooch in the shops. I still had an hour before I was due to meet Daniel.

Just as I walked past Café Rouge in the High Street, I heard someone call my name. I looked over the road and there was Tony waving at me. He crossed the road and came towards me.

'Hey, Lucy,' he said.

'Hi,' I said, blushing furiously. 'How are you?'

'Good. Are you still speaking to me, then?'

'Yeah, course.'

'I tried ringing you . . .'

'I know. Um, sorry . . .'

Tony looked around. 'So, what you doing?'

'Not much.' I showed him the bag with the cards in it. 'Just picked these up for Mum, then I was going to have a wander round the shops.'

'Let's go and get a drink and catch up, then,' he said, linking his arm through mine. 'I haven't seen you for ages.'

We found a table outside the Coffee Cup and he ordered a Coke, then asked what I'd like.

'Hot blackcurrant,' I said, thinking, Thank God I don't have to drink another of those awful espressos.

'You're looking good,' he said when the waitress had gone.

'So are you,' I said. 'Been out in the sun?'

He nodded. 'So, Nesta tells me that you have a new boyfriend.'

'Sort of. And you have a new girlfriend?'

'Sort of,' he said. 'Actually, no. That's over. Um, she doesn't know yet, though, I don't know how to tell her, but . . . nah, it's not working.'

'Why?'

Tony shivered and pulled a silly face. 'You know me, I'm not really into having the *big* relationship. You know, the world of coupledom. And she, well, she's getting a bit heavy, if you know what I mean. Always wanting to see me, like *every* day, and always phoning wanting to know what I am doing.'

'Too clingy?'

'*Yeah*, I feel like she's taking over my life.'

'Yeah,' I said.

'So how's it going with you and what's-his-name?'

'Daniel.' I shrugged. 'Not sure. I mean, it was great in the beginning, brilliant, but . . . I don't know, still early days. But same thing, really. He wants to do the couple bubble thing, just us in there. I don't know if I like it.'

Tony looked at me fondly. '*We* got on, though, didn't we?'

'We did.' I smiled back at him. 'And I'm sorry I over-reacted when you . . . you know, that evening in Highgate. I hope we can be mates.'

Tony put his hand on mine. 'You bet. Always. I tell you what, we'll be like Hugh Grant and Elizabeth Hurley. They used to go out and they're still best of friends.'

'Yeah,' I said. 'But you can be Liz and I'll be Hugh.'

Tony laughed. I'd forgotten how easy he was to be with. Fun. Not like Daniel, I thought. Everything was *so* intense with him. And so serious.

'So this new bloke is clingy, is he?' said Tony, looking pleased.

'Yeah. Always wanting to know what I'm doing, where I'm going. I feel like he's always checking up on me.'

'Like that boy over there,' said Tony. 'He's staring at you. You've got an admirer.'

I glanced over to where Tony was looking and my heart stopped. It was Daniel. And he didn't look happy.

I waved and beckoned him to come over, then introduced Tony. The two boys nodded at each other.

'Sit down,' I said. 'Join us.'

Daniel shifted about on his feet and seemed reluctant.

'Well, I was just off,' said Tony, getting up.

He leaned over and gave me a kiss on the cheek. 'See you soon, Lucy.' Then he left me, but as he walked away, he turned back and gave me a look as if to say, 'You're in trouble now, girl.'

He was right. Daniel took his seat and looked at me accusingly.

'So?' he said.

'So what?' I asked.

'Explanation?'

I didn't like his tone. 'For what?'

'You said you were doing a job for your mum, then I find you holding hands with some boy.'

'We weren't holding hands – well, not exactly. Tony's a mate. I haven't seen him for a while and we were catching up.'

'Didn't look like that from where I was,' said Daniel sulkily. 'It looked like you were really into each other.'

'I bumped into him when I came out of Rymans,' I said, thinking, Why am I feeling so defensive? 'Nothing was going on.'

'Yeah right,' said Daniel.

'You know what?' I said, getting up. 'You can think what you want.'

Daniel caught my hand and pulled me back down. 'No, sorry. Don't go, Lucy. It's just, well, it looked like you were having a really good time with him.'

'I was,' I said. 'But we're mates, that's all. Do you think you can't trust me or something?'

'I guess I just want you all to myself,' said Daniel, then grinned, 'and who can blame me? I guess I get jealous.'

'Well, there's no need.'

'No need, as long as you promise not to see him again.'

'*What*? No way. Anyway, he's Nesta's brother. I'll see him whenever I go to her house. Are you going to tell me I can't go there next?'

'No, but maybe I should go with you next time.'

I stood up again. 'You know what, Daniel? I don't think it's working with us. I don't like people telling me what to do all the time. And I don't like having to explain myself when I'm completely innocent. My friends mean a lot to me. And they include Tony, and if you don't like it, then too bad, because we're finished.'

And with that, I left him sitting there with his mouth hanging open. Ha, I thought. Put that in your designer pipe and smoke it.

When God made boys
She was only
joking

Dumpers and the Dumped

Instead of going home, I called Izzie. She was rehearsing with Ben near Highgate and was only too glad to have an excuse to get out for a break.

'Nesta's just called too. I said I'd see her in Raj's in half an hour,' she said.

On the way over to meet her, I began to have second thoughts about Daniel. Had I been too hasty? Mean? Heartless? Just finished with the best boy I would ever find? I hoped that Izzie would make me feel better about it all as it was my first experience of dumping someone.

As soon as Izzie appeared at Raj's, I filled her in on what had happened in the last week. It was such a relief to be able to talk freely to her again and I told her everything – what he'd been like when he came to my house and what had just gone on in Hampstead.

She looked shocked. 'How could he say that about your hair and your designs? You're brilliant. I reckon he's jealous, because he can see you have more talent than he's got in his little finger.'

'Anyway, I just finished with him,' I said.

'Good,' said Izzie. 'What a creepoid. He's like an emotional bully. What a control freak. But are you OK?'

I nodded. 'I think so. I don't know. I mean, some days we had a really good time. Maybe I shouldn't have been so hard on him. You know, with time, maybe I could have changed him.'

Izzie shook her head. 'My mum always says that the only time you can change a man is when he's a baby.'

I laughed. 'I guess. I was starting to feel like I had no space.'

'Like that joke,' said Izzie. 'Boys are like dogs – give them a bit of affection and they follow you everywhere.'

'Yeah right,' I said.

Izzie looked thoughtful. 'It's never easy being the dumper. You feel rotten.'

'Have you told Ben yet?'

'No. But I'm going to do it soon. I've been agonising over it for days. I don't know what I'm going to say. There's no easy way, is there?'

I thought back to how I'd told Daniel. 'Try, "We're finished." That says it all.'

'I guess,' said Izzie sadly. 'I hate having to do it.'

'Yeah. It's like, I think I made the right decision,' I said, 'but I feel mean.'

'So do I,' sighed Izzie, 'and I haven't even told him yet.'

At that moment, Nesta swept in and flopped down next to me.

'I've just been dumped,' she announced. 'Simon has dumped me. Me. *Me*.'

'Why? What happened?'

'I knew it was coming,' she said. 'I *told* you I knew it. He said he really liked me, blah blah, and that he hoped we could stay friends, blah blah, but because he was going to go to university, he felt it was a good idea that we made a clean break because it's a new chapter for him, blah blah, and that long distance relationships never work. Blah blah blah blah blah.'

'Are you very upset?' I asked.

'Over a boy? Course not. I don't care,' she said, and then she burst into tears, causing a lady on the next table to look over with concern. 'I *really* liked him, Lucy.'

'I know you did, Nesta. And I am sorry. Can I do anything? Get you anything?'

She shook her head. 'I'll be all right. Sorry. Sorry. Just I've never been dumped before.'

I went to sit next to her and put my arm around her. 'It's a day of firsts for both of us. I've just finished with Daniel.'

This seemed to cheer her up. 'Really? Good,' she said. 'I know I only met him once, but I didn't like him. I can say that now, can't I?'

'You can. You can say whatever you like.'

She wiped her eyes and attempted a smile. 'So here we are, the dumped and the dumper.'

'And Izzie's about to join the ranks,' I said.

'Ben?' said Nesta.

Izzie nodded. 'Boys,' she said. 'Who needs them?'

'Yeah,' said Nesta sadly, 'who?'

What is going on today? I thought, when I called in at home later. It must be something in the stars. In fact I'm surprised that Mystic Izzie hasn't picked up on some fight between planets or something which is provoking all our horoscopes. Everyone seems to be changing and rearranging their love life. Even my brother Lal was affected, and it takes a lot for him to change anything, even his socks.

'What's up with you?' I asked when I popped my head in the boys' room and saw him slumped on the bed *à la* tragic hero with his hand over his forehead.

'You wouldn't understand,' he said and turned away towards the wall.

'Try me,' I said. It wasn't like him to be low and even though he was a pain mostly, he was still my brother.

'I want to be alone,' he muttered.

I went in and sat on the end of his bed. 'I just finished with Daniel,' I said, in an attempt to perk him up. He usually couldn't resist the latest gossip about my and the other girls' love lives. Says it's good research.

Lal sat up. 'See, that's it, isn't it? You finished with Daniel. Another poor boy, subject to the whims and fancies of you girls.'

This wasn't the reaction I'd expected. 'What do you mean?'

'Girls,' he moaned. 'Can't live with them, can't shoot them. You can stick that on one of your T-shirts.'

'What *is* your problem?' I asked.

'Nothing,' he said. 'Girls. Or rather not girls. Sometimes it's not fair, you know. You girls call all the shots and us boys just have to take it.'

'Hey, what's happened to the snog chart?' I asked, noticing that the back of the door was bare.

'In the bin,' he said.

'Why? I thought you were winning.'

'I was. But what's the point? All those girls I've snogged and none of them meant anything to me.'

'But I thought that was the *point*. No ties, no commitment, just fun. I thought that was your philosophy.'

'Shows what *you* know,' he said.

'OK, so what is your philosophy, then?'

Lal sighed. 'I can't tell you. You'll laugh or tell your mates.'

'Trust me,' I said. 'I won't tell anyone.'

Lal sat up. 'OK. There's this girl. A girl I really fancy. I mean *really* fancy. I think she may be The One.'

'Well, that's good, isn't it? You've finally fallen for someone.'

'Not finally. I've fancied her for ages, but it's like she doesn't even know I'm on the planet,' he said. 'She barely even gives me a second glance.'

'So, make her notice you.'

'You think I haven't tried? No go. She'd never look at someone like me, she's way out of my league.'

He looked so sad sitting there, I wished I could do something to cheer him up. 'Hey, don't give up. It's not like you. Maybe I could help. Do I know her?'

Lal shook his head. 'No . . . Yes. I mean no.'

'Come on, spill. Who is it?'

Lal shook his head again. 'Can't say. See, you lot – you girls – you're all so self-assured. You, your mates, *all* girls, you don't realise how hard it is for us boys. You can destroy us with a look or with a comment that you all think is dead clever or funny and we're supposed to be all, Oh, it doesn't matter, ha ha, laugh at me why don't you?

But I've had enough. My ego is shattered. My life is over. There is no other girl but her and she'll never give me the time of day. *That's* why I ripped up the snog chart. I've been into this girl for ages. *Ages*. I thought if she saw how popular I was with other girls, she'd be intrigued, fancy me. But I don't think she's even noticed, so what's the point? Snogging a load of girls just to prove something to myself, that I'm fanciable, that girls can't resist me? What's the point when the only one that matters *can* resist me? I may as well be invisible as far as she knows.'

Wow, I thought. He's really got it bad. 'It can't possibly be that hopeless. I mean, you're a good-looking boy, you're a laugh. Perseverance wins the day. Come on. Who is it?'

He looked at the floor and then glanced up at me hopefully. 'Nesta.'

Ohmigod, I thought, he's right. No chance. *No* chance. He doesn't stand a hope in hell with her. Oh, poor Lal. It *is* hard being a boy. Poor Lal. Poor Daniel. And poor Ben – he's going to get it soon.

Falling in love is awfully simple.
Falling out of love is simply awful.

Chapter 17

Couple
Bubbles

Daniel wasn't about to give up easily.

Monday, he sent the most gorgeous white flowers. Through a proper florist as well.

Tuesday, another toy bear and a card saying, 'He's to go with little bear in case she's lonely.'

Wednesday, he phoned. 'Let's at least meet up, Lucy. Please. We can't just leave it.'

In the end, I agreed. I'd have felt mean not to. Nobody had ever sent me flowers before, not even Tony, and I felt at least I should hear him out.

'OK,' I said, 'but I'll come down to you.'

He was waiting for me at Chalk Farm tube and, as usual, was dressed in his signature black. He was carrying a small bunch of freesias. It was strange seeing him again. Even though it had only been a few days, he looked different. Or I was seeing him differently. No doubt he was good-looking, but this time, I felt the attraction had gone.

'Hi,' he said and took my hand.

'Hi,' I said and took it back.

'Oh, don't be like that, Lucy,' he said and gave me the flowers.

'Daniel, you can't keep giving me stuff. I mean, it's really lovely of you, but . . .'

'I wanted to get flowers for you. I want to be with you. To make you happy. I'm sorry about the other day. I was out of order. Can we give it another try? Start again?'

But I knew that it was over and shook my head. 'I'm sorry, Daniel.'

'But *why*? Was it because of the way I reacted to you being with that boy? I'm sorry. I get jealous. *Most* girls would like that.'

How could I let him down gently? 'It's not you, it's me. I want . . . that is, I don't want . . . I mean, I'm not . . .' I remembered what Tony had said. 'I'm not into having the big relationship. I mean, I think you're really lovely . . .'

Daniel's face clouded over. 'I know exactly what you're saying, Lucy. I'm not stupid. It's your choice. There are loads of other girls who would jump at the chance of going out with me.'

Good, I thought. Let them.

He reached for my hand again. 'One more try? I really think we've got something special.'

I shook my head. 'Sorry, Daniel. But . . . but I hope we can stay friends.' Argh. I was determined not to come out with that old cliché, but it slipped out.

'Yeah,' sighed Daniel. 'We all know what *that* means.'

'No, I mean it, we could still talk and even see each other sometimes, but as mates.'

'Yeah right,' he said.

I felt really uncomfortable as we both stood there staring at the pavement. I couldn't think of anything else to say and he seemed to have gone into a sulk.

'Well, er, um . . . I've got to go,' I said finally.

'Sure,' he said, and hung his head.

As I walked away, he just stood there looking after me. I felt like the Queen of Mean.

'What's up, Lucy?' Mum asked when I got back home later.

I sat down at the kitchen table and put my head in my hands. 'Relationships,' I said. 'They stink.'

Mum laughed. 'What's happened now? I thought it was all going brilliantly. We've hardly seen you for days, weeks.'

'Finished. History. *Kaput.*'

Mum sat next to me. 'Oh Lucy, I am sorry. You've been dumped.'

'No, *I* dumped *him*.'

'Oh,' said Mum. 'So, what's the problem?'

'It's just not worth it, any of it. Either way, love hurts. I feel mean, Nesta's been dumped and she feels lousy. Izzie wants to finish with Ben, but is worried about hurting him. And even Lal, he's in love with someone who'll never have him.'

'Nesta,' said Mum.

'How did you know?'

'You mean you've never noticed how he acts when she's around?'

'I thought he acted like that around all girls.'

Mum shook her head. 'No, he's got it bad for her.'

'Poor Lal,' I said. 'He's just not her type.'

'I know,' said Mum. 'It's hard to watch. I hate to see him pining, but *I* can't make her fancy him. What can you do?'

'Get a dog like TJ did,' I said.

Mum laughed again. 'We've already got Ben and Jerry. I don't know. I guess there's no point in me saying any of this to you, but I'm going to anyway. You *are* young. There will be others for all of you. Plenty more fish in the sea.'

'No,' I said. 'No point.'

Mum put her hand over mine. 'Life can be hard sometimes, Lucy, no matter what side you're on. It takes a lot of courage to finish with someone. Some people stay in bad relationships long after their sell-by date because they're too frightened to face the repercussions, but it's a good lesson to learn. You have to be cruel to be kind sometimes, especially if it's not working. If it ain't right, it ain't right. So why did you end it with Daniel?'

I shrugged. 'Dunno. It's like, I couldn't be myself with him. Like he wanted me to be someone else and was trying to mould me into that person, but it felt a bit like trying to fit a square peg into a round hole, you know? I didn't feel like we really fitted. Remember that day when you said that when the right person came along, you could be yourself with them, be natural?'

Mum nodded. 'But you're only fourteen, Lucy. So's Nesta. And Lal is only fifteen. Life goes on, and girls and boys will come and go. Sometimes it will be right, sometimes it will be wrong. Main thing is to stay true to yourself – to what you feel.'

'Well, Nesta feels awful. So does Lal.'

'Well, as I said, it's not always easy and I know this may sound weird to say, but all of you, *all* of you will be more understanding because of it. Nesta's never been dumped before, has she?'

I shook my head.

'Well, it doesn't hurt to be on that side of things; that

is, I know it *does* hurt, but it will give her more perspective and understanding. Boys fall over themselves for her, so perhaps having been dumped will make her a bit gentler on them. It's hard for boys sometimes.'

I nodded. 'That's what Lal said.'

'And Lal. Same with him. Knowing what it's like to have an almighty crush on someone who doesn't reciprocate, maybe he'll go easier on the girls that fancy *him* in future. He's had his fair share of girls queuing up for him in the past, and I've seen him act a bit ruthless with one or two of them.'

'Yeah, me too,' I said. 'I've seen him give girls the brush-off before and I thought he was being horrible, but now I feel like I misjudged him in a way. I thought he was an unfeeling rat, but really all he was trying to do was prove to himself that he was fanciable, because he felt insecure.'

'Exactly,' said Mum. 'All these experiences, they're all part of life's rich tapestry.'

'Yeah,' I said. 'I guess. But why can't it all be perfect? And everyone be happy. I hate seeing people feeling blue.'

Mum squeezed my hand. 'And that's what makes you Lucy. You may feel mean that you finished with Daniel, but it shows that you have a heart and that's what's most important. You care about people even if you can't change the situation. You ought to hear some of the stories some of my clients tell me about their relationships. Heartbreaking, some of them, and all I can do is listen and let them know that I'm there for them. That's all you can do with Nesta. And Lal.'

'Yeah,' I said. 'And Lal.'

I met TJ, Izzie and Nesta at Ruby's for dinner later that evening.

'Oh no,' said TJ. 'Now I'm the odd one out. Izzie's going to finish with Ben and you've finished with Daniel. I'm the only one with a boyfriend.'

Nesta grinned. 'Give it time.'

'Cynic,' said Izzie, punching her arm. 'Take no notice, TJ. You and Steve are lovely together. And at least he likes doing loads of different things.'

'Yeah,' said TJ. 'And we both have days when we do our own thing. He's not like . . he has to be with me all the time.'

'That's the secret,' I said as I looked at the menu. 'I mean, I know I haven't had many relationships, but I'm learning already. It's like, all of us did the same thing, except TJ of course. We all went into couple bubbles and cut ourselves off from each other and the rest of the world like nothing else existed.'

Nesta sighed. 'Yeah, but you can't help it when you're really into someone.'

'But there has to be balance,' I said. 'You see the boy, but you still see your mates. You do some stuff with the boy, some stuff with your mates and some stuff alone.'

'I guess,' said Nesta.

'Come on,' I said. 'Let's be positive. Let's celebrate our newfound freedom and order something to eat. All this dumping and being dumped, I'm starving.'

TJ and I ordered a big bowl of potato wedges with sour cream and chilli. Nesta ordered a hot chicken satay baguette and Izzie had a veg and halioumi kebab.

'Here's to the rest of the holidays,' said Nesta after the waitress had taken our orders.

'Yeah and here's to being single.' I smiled. 'It's so weird. I used to be, like, oh it's so rotten because I haven't got a boyfriend, and now I feel good about it. Like I'm free, no one to tell me what to do or who I can or can't see. Never again.'

'Oh no,' said Nesta, as a particularly good-looking boy came through the door and checked her out. 'You must *never* say never. Not all boys are like Daniel, Lucy. He was very possessive. I'm glad you stood up to him in the end.'

'OK,' I laughed. 'I'll never say never, then. But I do say, here's to mates. Look how everything's changed since the beginning of the hols, but here we all are, still together. Boys may come in our lives . . .'

'Oh, I hope so,' interrupted Nesta as the boy who'd

eyed her up sat at the next table. 'Look out boys, Nesta's back in town.'

'As I was saying,' I continued. 'Boys may come *and* go in our lives. Sometimes we'll have boyfriends, sometimes we won't, but we'll always have each other. So I say, here's to mates.'

'Arr, she's *so* sweet,' teased Izzie. 'Little bear.'

'Little *bear*,' chorused TJ and Nesta, then laughed.

'Naff off, dorkbrains,' I said. 'But it's true, mates always have each other. I say we celebrate properly. I'll ask my mum if we can have a party on Friday. A no-boyfriends-allowed party. You can only come if you're single.'

Nesta's face dropped. 'No boys? Are you sure?'

'Yes Nesta, I'm sure. Everyone's so different when there are boys around. Let's have a night off from them. We can invite some of the girls from school.'

'Yeah,' said Izzie. 'It'll be brilliant to spend some time with just the girls.'

'That's settled, then,' I said. 'I'll ask Mum.'

Party
Time

Mum couldn't believe it when at last I fulfilled my promise to cook for the family. She agreed to let me have the party, so I phoned around and found out everyone's favourite comfort food in times of Relationship Trouble. Then I did a practice run the night before to make sure I had it perfected.

> *Party menu:*
> *Doritos and salsa dips*
> *Oven chips*
> *Pizza*
> *Sausages*
> *Chocolate bars*
> *Ice cream (assorted, loads)*

'This cooking lark is quite simple, really,' I said, as I took the oven chips out of the oven and put them on the table.

'Er,' said Mum, 'it is when you buy ready-to-serve stuff like this.'

'Yeah,' said Steve. 'For your information, potatoes actually come in their own skin and you have to peel them.'

'Ha ha,' I said. 'But oven chips were big in the popularity stakes and I can't say you seem that bothered, seeing as you've just eaten three at once.'

'I think you lot had better get boyfriends again quick,' said Dad, helping himself, 'or else we're all going to be as fat as pigs.'

'Mum, can Lucy cook every night from now on?' asked Lal through a mouthful of chips and ketchup.

'No,' said Mum. 'All this pre-packaged stuff may taste great, but it isn't too healthy. You know what I say – you are what you eat.'

'In that case, you're a Nettuno pizza,' I laughed as I noticed that she'd cleared her plate and had even gone for a second helping.

The girls and I all got dressed at my house on the night of the party and we took ages doing each other's nails and make-up. We decided to get dressed up even though there weren't going to be boys there. We did it for ourselves, just for the fun of it, as sometimes getting dressed up is the best part of any party. It felt great just to hang out with the girls again and Nesta seemed to be in better spirits, despite her recent dumping. For the first time in weeks I felt myself again. Calm inside, on an even keel instead of on the rollercoaster of emotions. Being single is OK, I decided, as I watched Nesta rolling about on the floor, zipping herself into an impossibly tight pair of jeans, especially when you have such good mates.

I'd thought very carefully about what to do on the Big Night. I wanted everyone to have loads of fun with lots to do. I hate those boring parties where everyone stands around in cliques just talking and watching each other. My plan was:- a bit of dancing, a video to watch while we ate (*Bridget Jones's Diary,* of course), then games and maybe some more dancing.

When everyone was ready, I thought I'd better break a bit of news about the party that I hadn't already told them. I had invited a boy.

'Um, just one thing before we go downstairs,' I said. 'You know this is a singles' party?'

The girls all nodded.

'Well, single doesn't necessarily mean all female, does it?'

'No,' said Nesta, looking at me suspiciously.

'I have invited *one* boy,' I said. 'Only one.'

'Tony,' said Nesta. 'Oh, Lucy . . .'

'No, not Tony.' I grinned.

'Oh, not *Daniel*,' exclaimed Izzie. 'I can't believe you've got back with him.'

I shook my head. 'No . . .'

Just at that moment, there was a knock, and the bedroom door opened. The girls all burst out laughing. A vision of girlie loveliness appeared in the doorway wearing my inflatable bra over his T-shirt and one of Mum's hippie wigs from the dressing-up box.

'Hi,' said Lal. 'I'm Lalita.'

'He's an honorary girl for the night,' I explained. I knew it would be a fantasy come true for him to be alone in a house full of girls and I really wanted to cheer him up. I thought it might help him get over his unrequited love for Nesta.

He wiggled into the room, sat on the bed and crossed his legs gracefully. 'So,' he pouted, splaying out his fingers, 'what do you think? Pink nail polish or purple?'

Half an hour later some of the guests began to arrive. Gabby, Jade, Mo and Candice from school; Amy, who lives next door to Izzie and has just bust up with her boyfriend; and TJ's second cousin who's never had a boyfriend and was very happy to come and celebrate being single.

'Music for singletons,' said Amy, showing us her rucksack full of CDs. She put a CD in the player and soon we were all dancing away to 'Survivor' by Destiny's Child, then we sang 'All by Myself' by Celine Dion at the top of our voices. After a good bop to more CDs, Izzie, Lal and I served the food and we all sat on the floor in the living room to watch *Bridget Jones*. I felt so relaxed to be there just with mates. I could tell everyone felt the same. Not having to worry about what was going to happen or how things were going to turn out. What this boy said or didn't say, who that boy was dancing with and who he wanted to snog. No expectations, no disappointments.

'So what games shall we play?' asked Izzie as the credits rolled after the movie.

'We could play Spin the Bottle, but with forfeits instead of snogging,' I said. 'Whoever spins the bottle has to set the forfeit, and whoever the bottle points at has to do it.'

Everyone seemed keen to give it a go, so Nesta found a bottle and got things started. We all sat cross-legged in a circle and began. It was hysterical, as everyone seemed to take it as an opportunity to make their friends act really stupid. Izzie made TJ do an impersonation of Madonna, so when it was TJ's turn, she asked Izzie to do an impression of drunk snake. Candice asked Nesta to do a cartwheel and Nesta asked Candice to run out into the garden and sing 'God Save the Queen' at the top of her voice.

I already had an idea for when it came to my turn. I spun the bottle slowly to my left, and just as planned, it stopped at Nesta.

'So Nesta,' I said. 'All those complaints about no boys at the party ... As your friend, I had to listen to what you really wanted so your forfeit is ... to snog my brother Lal in the hall.'

Nesta looked over at Lal, who was holding his breath. She raised an eyebrow. 'Do you think he could take it?' she asked.

'I'll take the chance,' he said.

He looked like all his Christmases had come at once when she stood up, took his hand and led him out of the room.

After a few minutes he came back in and had to go and lie down on the sofa to recover. I swear there were stars and planets coming out of his head.

'So what about you and Tony now?' asked TJ as we cleared some of the dishes back into the kitchen.

I shrugged. He had phoned in the morning, probably hoping to get an invite to our party. It was weird, because at the end of the call, he sounded uncertain, then asked if maybe we could pick up where we left off at the beginning of the holidays. I told TJ about it.

'So what did you say?'

'I said I couldn't. I mean, to pick up where we were at the beginning of the holidays? All that uncertainty? No thanks. Amazing, huh? A few weeks ago I would have leapt at the chance, but so much has happened since then – since my letter to him, since Daniel. I feel I need some time out to think about things . . . to reassess what I want. To go back to where I was at the beginning of summer, to the ups and downs and wondering what was happening with Tony . . .? If I said, "OK, let's get back together," how long would it last? I know what he's like. He gets bored and then where would that leave me? Back on the rollercoaster. I'm not sure I want to go through all that again. Not yet.'

'Sounds like a very wise decision,' said TJ. 'No hurry.'

'No, no hurry,' I said. 'We can be friends for sure, but I just don't want a commitment relationship.'

'Sounds like you were made for each other.'

I laughed and followed her back into the living room where some of the girls from school were urging Izzie to get up and sing. At first she was reluctant, then she smiled. 'Actually I have been working on a new song . . .'

Everyone started stomping their feet and shouting, 'Izzie, Izzie, Izzie.'

'OK,' she said. 'This one is for all the singletons.' She

closed her eyes for a few seconds, then began to sing in her lovely, velvety voice.

I was a broken ship with ragged sails
Now calm waters beckon me
Lying out in warming sun, stretching, feeling free
Waiting for a new wind and a wave upon my bow
Wishing on a rainbow, following my star
Welcoming my new world, I'm gonna travel far

Floating in the slip-stream, just going with the flow
Booked a passage on tomorrow with no one else in tow
Floating in the slip-stream, just going with the flow.

I glanced over at TJ and she smiled back. Going with the flow, I thought. Yeah, now *that* sounds good to me.

The MATES, DATES series
by Cathy Hopkins:

1. Mates, Dates and Inflatable Bras

2. Mates, Dates and Cosmic Kisses

3. Mates, Dates and Portobello Princesses

4. Mates, Dates and Sleepover Secrets

5. Mates, Dates and Sole Survivors

6. Mates, Dates and Mad Mistakes

7. Mates, Dates and Pulling Power

8. Mates, Dates and Tempting Trouble

9. Mates, Dates and Great Escapes

10. Mates, Dates and Chocolate Cheats

11. Mates, Dates and Diamond Destiny

Companion book: Mates, Dates Guide to Life

The TRUTH, DARE, KISS OR PROMISE series
by Cathy Hopkins:

1. White Lies and Barefaced Truths

2. Pop Princess

3. Teen Queens and Has-Beens

4. Starstruck

5. Double Dare

6. Midsummer Meltdown

Find out more at www.piccadillypress.co.uk